For my beloved sister, the eternal Michelle Gonzalez Green.
May your ancestral fire bring radiance to the archipelagoes beyond the sky.

content warnings

Natural Disaster, Colonialism, Assimilation, Racism, Transphobia, Character Death, Depictions of PTSD/Trauma, Depiction of Mental Illness, Carceral Interrogation, Violence.

Sordidez

E.G. Condé

Stelliform Press
Hamilton, Ontario

Table of Contents

•

jurakán | heart of sky

"The most ultimately righteous of all wars is a war with savages ... the rude, fierce settler who drives the savage from the land lays all civilized mankind under a debt to him."

Theodore Roosevelt, *The winning of the West*, 1889 CE

It was after dusk when Teddy came for us. His breath was thick and wet as it swept through the forest. Not even the coquis dared to chirp with him there, rummaging in the brush. I can still remember the wails of the trees as he flayed their barks, as he dismembered them limb by limb.

I was huddled with my family when his tongues slithered through cracks in our zinc roof, bored holes in the tarp that we hoped would shield us. Someone screamed when the roof caved in, splintered under the weight of a fallen yabisi. Its pale trunk cracked like bone beneath his invisible fist. Then, Teddy descended, jaws bared, his saliva oozing down on us in wicked rivulets.

Hands clasped, we pleaded to our creator for quick deaths. But death never came. Instead, as if our cemís had heard our prayers,

Teddy's voice caught in his throat. Silence. It was as if the engine of the cosmos had suddenly shuttered its industry, giving way to quiet entropy. And that's when I remembered what the Gobernadora had said on the radio the night before, her warning not to trust the stillness. "No habrá paz en medio de la tormenta."

When it was so quiet that I could hear my heart drumming in my ears, I clambered out of the wreckage. My sisters cursed at me for my foolishness, but soon they followed, curious. Where the roof had collapsed, bleached bark and serrated metal parted like the petals of a hideous flower to reveal him, grinning and gordo in the pallid sky. Below, the jungle had withered to a tangle of brown, as if his breath curled with unseen flame. A coconut palm whined and crashed. Its death echoed over the mountains, twisting into something that reminded me of laughter. I lifted my gaze to the sky to search for the face of the Taíno deity that legends say takes the shape of a storm, arms curling like serpents to set the clouds into a devastating spiral. Jurakán.

Teddy was the twentieth of twenty-two names randomly assigned for that year by the National Oceanic and Atmospheric Administration. But I like to think that he was named after the Teddy, the American conquistador, the last to lay claim to this little jewel in the Caribbean I call home. How fitting that he should be the one to usher in the end of American dominion here. Perhaps we should be grateful. Some pray that our new masters will be better caretakers of our land, but we jíbaros have our doubts.

I regret not taking Mandarin at university as we sift through the packages our new rulers airdrop for us. Bags of rice. Insulin. Antibiotics. Distilled water. Bioprinted protein powder. Will the Chinese be more sympathetic than their American or Spanish predecessors? They are not strangers to our suffering. They must remember when their people were sent here as laborers to work in the factories, that last ditch effort to save Spain's crumbling empire with industry. Or when the Americans' Chinese Exclusion Act uprooted thousands from their communities, leaving them few refuges other than our colonial backwater. What an irony that the ones the Spanish and the Americans spat on and called coolies ended up as our new landlords.

The US sold us off like a bad investment. But on the radio they said that the Americans were on the verge of bankruptcy, that the Chinese seized Puerto Rico as collateral for unpaid debts. The price for defaulting on too many climate loans. I applaud the Chinese for banking on our collective apathy to curb emissions to win out in the end. With this International Climate Bank, they hold all the cards now. Financing natural disaster recovery efforts. Cementing their global influence by sowing debt. Before Teddy, the talking heads said that their President should get it over with and declare himself Emperor. Emperor of what, I wonder? After COVID-19, Androvirus, the gigafires and heat domes, the Thwaites Ice Shelf and Teddy, who wants to rule a world that is half-underwater and half-scorched to a dustbowl?

After Teddy, I had to teach myself not to care about what happens beyond my shores, even if that is what I spent my life preparing to do. I ignore what I hear about the Yucatán, parched by chemical weapons into a desert by the madman elected to care for it. I ignore accounts of drones slaughtering civilians branded as 'apostates' in Siberia for opposing the Tsarina's theocratic regime. I ignore the latest updates on this Sino-American cold war with many fronts, fought by many proxies. It feels silly, my dream of being a journalist, that noble reporter who covered these last days of 'civilization.' Teddy had other plans for me. Now I'm here in the mountains, weaving solar nets with my sisters.

"It's like when I used to braid your hair, Vero," my little sister

Yuíza says, showing me how to entwine kapok fibers, strands of blue tarp, cables, copper filaments, bulbs and glittering fragments of solar panels. She hands me a basket of materials. Her dimples are little caverns that deepen with delight. Yuíza. Ever the optimist.

I set the basket on top of a ladder and begin to thread a mesh of fibers through the boughs of a gnarled fig tree. "Remember when I did your hair for your Quinceñeara?"

Anacaona bursts into laughter behind me. My elder twin, the serious one. Even she cracks at the memory. "How could anyone forget?"

Our mother was running late that day, like always. Deciding that the fifteen kilograms of arroz con gandules she had prepared wouldn't be enough to feed the dozen people she was expecting, she went to the market at the last minute for more pork, plantains, breadfruit and God knows what else. Anacaona, our mother's shadow, was recruited for the shopping trip, leaving Yuíza and I behind. What was I to do? The princesa needed to be ready for her big moment. I did what I could, which admittedly was far from adequate. I'll never forget Mami's screams of disgust upon her return, how she wrenched the comb from my hands as if it were a murder weapon. The arcane arts of the feminine have always eluded me.

"On second thought, maybe you can help Dagüao with the breakers," Yuíza says gently, her black curls falling over her face as she peers down at me from a rooftop.

"It's coming along." Anacaona gestures toward the forest, eyes alight with pride as she repositions her ladder.

I help Dagüao with the labyrinth of switches and breakers he built behind the cancha, the ballcourt that has become our unofficial town square. He's another genius like Yuíza. Which explains why they've been best friends since they could crawl. I remove a rusted screw and grab a cable to attach to the open switch when I catch an expression of alarm in Dagüao's green eyes.

-Not that!- he signs, the pads of his index and middle fingers clamping to that of his thumb.

I make a circle with my fist over my heart to reply. -Sorry.-

Dagüao passes me the end of another cable wrapped around his shoulder. I socket it into place and retighten the screws. Dagüao grins with approval, tucking his black hair into an elastic tie. In his delicate smile lines and sharp cheekbones, I can see the ghost of his father's face, an artisan and mechanic from Ponce who moved to our mountains to build a new life with others who could communicate in his language. Teddy took too many of us.

When you're raised in the campo, hearing or not, you learn to sign if you want to understand what's going on. In primary school we learned a bit of ASL. But our neighbors speak a regional dialect of their own, sometimes specific to families. Communication is not the most straightforward up here, but you get used to it — you have to. We hearing people regularly switch from Spanish to English to Spanglish to ASL and LSPR and ASLPRish and that resurrected Island Arawak that youth learn at summer camp.

Dagüao riffles through a shipping container filled with useful scrap, searching for solar batteries to attach to his contraption. I follow him with discarded cable shielding and copper thread and drop them into bins that he has meticulously labeled to keep our salvage organized.

In the months since Teddy, we became scavengers to survive. They don't tell you that the aftermath of the storm is the worst part. They don't tell you about the despairing nights, praying for help that never comes. About digging mass graves to bury the dead under the smog-choked skies of diesel generators.

In the end, we endured as we always have. Like the petroglyphs of frogs and birds etched in boulders along our rivers. We endured. From the debris of our towns, we created this yucayeke, this mountain sanctuary that has served many generations of our ancestors, going back to those daring Taíno and Yoruba that settled here, to escape the reach of the Spanish crown that enslaved them.

But with our kerosene supply dwindling, we had to find a new way to keep the lights on. Even though Teddy's Category 6 winds shattered most of the island's solar panels, Yuíza schemed a way to remake the debris into something that might save us. For all that our isla lacks, we have sunshine in abundance. So we weave the reflective shards of solar panels with kapok fibers from our sacred ceiba trees. We stitch circuits into a meshwork that we drape over the branches. We make solar microgrids with life's stringy filaments. We call them our *nasa* — an Arawak word for the nets that our ancestors used to catch fish in our seas and rivers, when they were still teeming with life.

"Y la música?" Anacaona descends from the ladder, the glossy twists of her hair swaying past her hips. She crosses her arms, her broad shoulders and tall stature instantly commanding respect. "It's too quiet."

At her bidding, Don Brizuela wheels onto the scene, followed by his grandchildren, Alonsito and Enriquillo. They carry maracas, guiros, panderetas, and his twelve-stringed pride and joy, a cautro he named *India Encantada*, to honor his late wife. The children guide him onto the raised catwalk we built for him to get around the village, but he has already mastered the makeshift ramps.

"How about something more retro than Bad Bunny?" He chuckles beneath his threadbare sombrero. The band strikes up an old folk song called "Espérame En El Cielo."
"Wait for me in heaven, my love,
If you are the first of us to go,
Wait for me, because soon, I will come,
To where you are, beyond the sky.
Between bales of cloud as soft as cotton.
Where we will live again."
Dagüao notices the tears in my eyes. His hands stack and then part like a square, lips curling to mirror my sorrow. -Sad?-

I feign laughter as I sign, -Estoy bien.-

I tell him I'm fine but I'm not. None of us are. I pretend as I have every day since that wall of mud buried our house with Mami, Papi, and Abuela Serafina inside, the day we became orphans and my dreams for the future were washed away. The day our community's survivors turned to us, the children of their deceased pastor, for leadership.

Anacaona's nails gently scratch my shoulder. She has never been the sentimental type, but I recognize this warm gesture. She always knows what I'm feeling. It's a twin power, our grandfather used to say. "Ready?"

Yuíza and Dagüao huddle in anticipation, eager to see if their mad science experiment will end in disaster or triumph. -Turn on the lights- they sign in unison. They look like magicians pulling rabbits out of hats.

We grab the ignition cord together, and the generator sputters to life.

The forest flickers. Like neon spiderwebs woven across the canopy, our solar nets activate. It's as if a thousand fireflies are frozen in amber above our yucayeke, their light softening everything as dusk falls. The cheers are hesitant at first, skeptical even. But after a minute or so of uninterrupted power, I jump up to hug Anacaona, shouting in that excited way I used to when we were kids. Don Brizuela is drumming his pandereta. Dagüao kisses Yuíza. Alcimar stares up in disbelief, removing his cap. The children clap and cheer and some of them run to their tents to fetch tablets to charge, followed closely by the stray dogs that have become their protectors. Grateful to be able to read his book late into the evening, Don Mateo drops into his hammock. Doña Marta switches on the electric grill, her daughter already prepping iguana kebabs and toasted casabe for the celebration.

Anacaona tosses me one of our last medallas. I snap open the can with care, as if handling a prized vintage. Teddy taught me not to take small pleasures for granted. "Salud!" I say to her, raising my can to hers. Her eyes sparkle as we tip our cans to our lips. The drink is still sweet well after expiry.

"For the yucayeke!" She twirls in a circle with her can raised.

"I thought you didn't like calling it that."

"This isn't Taíno summer camp, Vero. But I think grandfather would be proud of what we've built here. The nasa, the yucayeke."

I take a swig from my can. "Oh, Abuelo Abey! I'm sure he's looking up at us from hell right now. Yeah, that's what you get for worshipping idols!" I shout, mimicking my mother's angry exchanges with her eccentric father.

Anacaona chuckles and crushes her empty can. "Mami was too harsh on him. Never forgave him for naming me and hermanita after old Taíno chiefs."

I grab Anacaona's empty as I finish my own and toss them in the salvage bin. "I think she believed in that stuff once." Our mother never stopped me from visiting Abuelo Abey's bohío, where he showed me the striking faces of the elder gods etched in stone. I remember being frightened by their cavernous eyes, like the orbital sockets of skulls. "It unsettled her ... the possibility that her God was only one of many."

Anacaona scoffed. "Meanwhile our father and his mother were doing Santería in our basement. She let that slide. As long as they have the names of saints." Anacaona searches the crowd, spotting Dagüao and Yuíza approaching from the grill. The smell that precedes them is smoky and delicious.

"Los pinchos están listos!" Yuíza passes me a stick of charred, greasy meat.

Dagüao smiles as his clenched fist drums his open palm. -Buen provecho.-

I nod gratefully, then devour Doña Marta's famous pincho. As dusk falls on the mountains and the frogs begin to sing, we drink and feast on iguana kebabs, breadfruit fritters, and crumbly casabe. There is laughter. The children are playing gallitos in the cancha. They giggle and cheer as they toss algarroba seeds threaded through string.

For a moment I allow this contagion of hope to lift me up. Somehow we always find joy, even when everything is taken from us. Even when we live in rubble and so many of us have vanished. For a moment, all I can feel is the love and warmth radiating from the faces of my community. And then I remember the shadow that looms over it all.

As the night deepens, as the people drink and grow bolder, their joy will sour. Even after this miracle we built for them, they'll whisper and jeer. They'll laugh and point behind my back. Because they know who I was. And they hate this new me. Just like Mami and Papi. I feel it in my bones.

But tonight I am spared. One by one, every phone, tablet, and computer lights up. An SOS on the emergency alert system. Another crisis. Another opportunity to make a difference. They'll be too busy needing me to judge.

The next morning the yellow-eyed changos are screeching like monkeys. Dagüao and Yuíza are in the workshop fiddling with radio equipment, trying to parse a signal. Some people are packing. Others are complacent, uncertain of what to do. The children are oblivious, climbing in trees like monitos, while their canine protectors roam in circles, whining. Dogs know things. They know the danger we're in. I reread the message for the tenth time, as if the act will invoke some stroke of brujería that will amend our fate.

"You have a choice," I say, and the bickering elders quiet.

Alcimar, the built-like-an-ox son of a carpenter, emerges from the crowd. He scratches the cleft of his chin. "And what brilliant idea do you have this time? For someone so educated you really are foolish."

"Watch your mouth!" Anacaona's rage hardens every syllable.

Alcimar points to the canopies, his arms as thick as their branches. "The lights are cute. But cute isn't going to save us. Cute isn't going to feed us, now that the Chinese are evicting us. No supply drops for squatters. Time to evacuate."

"We can stay," I stammer. The crowd is hushed. "If we are brave enough. Doña Marta's conucos are thriving, we could plant more, grow enough to sustain ourselves. And Dagüao's cisterns catch enough of the rainfall. The biogas —"

Alcimar bursts into laughter. "You think because your madre was Doña Ines that gives you the right to tell people what to do? You think because you went to uni you're smarter than the rest of us? You think because you built this ridiculous 'yucayeke' that makes you some kind of caci███—"

"Cacique," Anacaona interjects, referring to the traditional Taíno chief, a man who inherits power from his maternal lineage. He would have misgendered me if she hadn't stopped him.

"Whatever," Alcimar sneers, ignoring Anacaona. "We can't keep chanting pa'lante and hope everything works out. This isn't one of your news stories for *Nuevo Día*. This is real life. I won't let you lead these people to their graves. We've buried too many already."

I know he isn't done. I resist the urge to close my eyes against what I know is coming.

"You're not fooling anyone. Stop pretending you're someone you're not. It's time we cut our losses."

There it is. I go for the jugular. "Remind us what you did after Teddy."

Tears brighten Alcimar's eyes. "I went to clear the road — find help."

"Mentiroso!" Anacaona pushes through the crowd and leans in an inch from Alcimar's face. My breath catches on a familiar mix of envy and admiration for my twin. She grabs the collar of his shirt. "You tried to run."

"I —" Alcimar stammers, his lips quivering.

"You were afraid," I say gently. "We all were. But in the end you made a choice to come back. You chose to give this yucayeke a chance. It's not much, but it's ours."

Don Brizuela stirs in his wheelchair. "But how, muchachos, how can we survive without the Chinese crates?"

-There's still lots of salvage,- I sign. "And we can grow our own food and medicine. I know many of you remember the old ways, the ways of your grandparents and theirs. So teach us. Teach us how to tend the conucos, how to grow and cut the yuca with the moon. Teach us the memory." I pause to restate myself in sign, watching Doña Marta's face spark with recognition. -And then we can teach the others.-

"The others?" Alcimar asks, defeat still heavy in his look.

Anacaona steps into the crowd. This time, I interpret as she speaks. "All over the archipelago there are others like us who think they have no choice but to agree to these eviction terms. If we do nothing, they'll end up as construction monitors for the drones rebuilding our coastlines. Or worse, they'll sign relocation contracts and get shipped off to a flotilla in the South China Sea."

Dagüao and Yuíza return from the rusty shipping container we call the workshop. Their eyes are wide as they take in the confrontation. Above me, the leaves of a weeping Yabisi whisper.

"If we expand our network, if we work with other communities — pool resources — we have a better chance of surviving."

"But how can we reach them?" Don Mateo says from the folds of his hammock, his voice the crisp basso of a retired radio host. "They've cut the fiber. And last I checked the radio waves are scrambled to prevent American spies from contacting the mainland. We'd need serious broadcast capability."

Yuíza raises a hand. -We have an idea- she signs as she speaks, winking at Dagüao.

Anacaona lets out an exaggerated sigh. "If only the Americans hadn't recently abandoned an enormous piece of radio infrastructure."

"It's a pile of ruins in the jungle by now." Don Mateo grumbles, as he leans back in the hammock.

"Don't get too comfortable, tío," I say. "You're coming with us."

"I'm what?" Don Mateo rises, a rare display of interest.

"We'll get the caballos ready," Alonsito says.

Dagüao shrugs out of Yuíza's clutches and steps into the center of the crowd. With a grin on his face, he taps his right shoulder with the fingers of his opposite hand, strafing it across his chest before allowing it to rest at his side. I recognize this as the sign for *king*. But everyone knows what he means by that.

"Cacique," they sign and chant, eyes fixed on me.

"Alcimar will come around," Yuíza says as we veer north along the splintered asphalt that was once Carretera 10.

"I hope so," I say, easing my grip on the reins. The old mare slows to a gentler trot, anticipating the uneven terrain. "He's a huge help when he isn't such a pendejo."

"And you have a crush on him," Anacaona teases from behind. I don't need to look back to see her suggestively lilting eyebrows.

"I do not," I lie through clenched teeth.

Don Mateo takes point, with Dagüao and Alcimar close behind. We trudge along the seams of asphalt that are slowly being reclaimed by the jungle. Mud and roots erupt through the gaps, buckling the ground. Beyond these rugged hills looms the cordillera. A crown of green minarets lifting toward the tropical sky, thick with ceibas and tors of golden karst. I used to hike up to those limestone formations with my grandfather, searching for caves where the ancient Taíno scrawled images of their gods onto the guano-stained walls.

We reach the observatory just before dusk. It looks different than the last time I was here, a first grader on a field trip. We came to marvel at this technological pearl the Americans built in our jungle to surveil the stars for messages from other worlds. The fading white girders, sunken platform, and bones of the satellite dish are netted with leafy webs of cissus verticillate. The raised catwalks that once encircled the complex have partially collapsed. The jungle hungers to be rid of the memory of this portal to the cosmos.

Alcimar secures the horses, eyeing me as he does it. I wonder if he has overheard my sisters' teasing. I dismount, noticing that the others are already sifting through their packs. I take a deep breath, still nervous to be alone with him after our confrontation.

"Hey, about earlier —" Alcimar scratches his buzzed hair beneath his Yankees cap. "I shouldn't have. I'm sorry."

I punch his shoulder in response, smirking. "Don't be a cabrón, okay?"

He smiles back, rubbing his shoulder, his look lingering.

I leave him to scout ahead with Anacaona, mostly to reassure a spooked Yuíza that no chupacabras have taken up residence in the ruins. The entrance to the complex is collapsed, the ceiling pocked with holes. We navigate the halls, ducking in places where the roof sags. We reach the main control room for the radio telescope, partially dismantled since the Americans abandoned their dreams of interstellar empire. There are stacks of receiver equipment, rusty servers, disk drives, and analog dials I can't make sense of. I catch Anacaona staring at the faded National Science Foundation logo still visible on the wall beneath a smudged American flag.

"We should make the change in management official." She winks, revealing the can of spray paint in her left hand. She gives it a shake, and the metal ball inside rattles like a maraca. This is her anthem, a music that means genesis. She closes her eyes, listening to the tree frogs for inspiration. When she opens her eyes again, she works quickly, creating two gold islands with separate strokes. Then, with a third stroke she draws a limber body and webbed legs. Just like that the NSF symbol is overtaken by a coqui. We are so mesmerized by the dripping gold paint that we don't hear the others coming.

-Cute-, Dagüao signs, appraising the new logo.

Anacaona blows him a kiss, her clumsy sign for -thank you.-

After several hours of wrangling with cables, solar batteries, and extensions, our crew has repurposed the ruined infrastructure to suit our needs. Don Mateo is recording frequencies on a notepad, circling candidates for a broadcast. With pencil poised, he listens for military chatter.

"Whatever message we send, expect it to be intercepted by the Chinese."

"Then we'll need to send our message in code," Yuíza jots down prime numbers and morse code.

Alcimar jumps, startled by Dagüao who emerges from an under-floor plenum, cables snaked over his shoulders. I catch him up on our discussion. -Any ideas?- I sign.

-Not numbers.-

-Why not?-

-They have computers.-

Yuíza sighs. "He's right. Their algos will crack whatever code we come up with."

Anacaona tilts her head toward her coqui glistening on the wall. Even through the observatory walls, the music of the tree frogs is a constant. The tiny bachelors trumpet their eligibility, hoping to entice a mate with the vigor of their performance.

I understand Anacaona's gesture. "Summer camp."

My twin smirks. "Summer camp."

Yuíza and Dagüao stare blankly at me and my sister. Don Mateo adjusts his glasses on his nose. Alcimar shakes his head, suppressing a laugh.

"Guaitiao!" I say in the old language. An ancient greeting ceremony, one that turns strangers into family.

"Guaitiao!" Yuíza repeats excitedly as she spells the word for Dagüao.

Don Mateo claps. "Very clever. They won't expect an extinct language."

Yuíza nods. "An extinct and undocumented language."

"Like the Navajo Code Talkers," Don Mateo says.

I relay our plan to Dagüao who readies the broadcast equipment, while Don Mateo hones in on an open frequency.

Anacaona hands me the headset. "You were always better at speaking it."

"You're sure?"

"Yes." Anacaona bows her head mockingly. "My cacique."

"You're making fun of me."

"It's my right. Respect your elders."

"You're barely five minutes older than me."

"And that makes me five minutes wiser."

I scoff, pulling the headset on. "What should I say?"

"You wanted to be a reporter, didn't you?"

"Okay," I sigh, tapping the microphone.

Don Mateo gives me a thumbs up.

All eyes on me, I take a deep breath. I think back to summer camp. To weekends with Abuelo Abey in the selva, at the ceremonial parks and archaeological sites of our Indigenous forebears. "The Taíno live on in you now," he used to say. I shut my eyes and begin Guaitiao, the exchange of names.

It's been a year since our yucayeke became a cacicazgo, since our village became one of many. Cut off from Chinese supply drops, we've learned self-reliance. Between Doña Marta's conucos, the chickens we found in Guayanilla, and trading with the Orocovis, Coamo, Canóvanas, and Gurabo yucayekes in the east and Maricao in the west, we're seldom hungry. But medicine and tech are a different story. Doña Juana is our resident curandera, but her santiguar massages and ratero oil only get us so far. Last month, we had to ferry Don Manolo to Ponce, the enemy's southern stronghold, to keep him from falling into a diabetic coma. We said our goodbyes, accepting that we would never see him again, else risk being arrested.

The Chinese have ceded the mountains to us for now. On the radio, our Chino-Boricua informers in the city tell us that the Chinese are strained for resources, that their war with the Americans is about to go hot. We hear they have blockaded New York's harbor, demanding repayment for climate debts.

Their distraction is an opportunity. We push deeper into the urban perimeter, daring to go as far north as Arecibo and as far west as Rincón, raiding the abandoned mansions of cryptobarons for tech, medicines, and good booze. I remember when they first settled our islands' coasts, gringos with appropriated hairstyles wearing multi-colored suits or vaguely Indigenous robes to cast them as good capitalists. In the beginning, they invited our communities to join their cultish self-help meetings, where they touted crypto as the pathway to freedom for all "mankind." Their promised land came in the form of luxury condos and sweeping gentrification that displaced most of the Boricuas that lived there. They ate well in this tax haven.

But now the tables have turned.

Anacaona is having too much fun tagging their neighborhoods

with inky vulgarities. In the tumultuous days before Teddy, when we infiltrated their cult meetings and heckled them at their fancy hotels and convention centers, when our people marched on San Juan to demand the end of American rule, some of them packed up and left, afraid for their lives when the protests got "violent" and the Feds came to remind us that we were theirs. The last of them were gone hours before Teddy made landfall.

This afternoon, my sisters and I enjoy some plundered cognac. We sit on our dujos, the children's plastic stools we like to think of as our thrones. Yuíza elaborates on the Taíno-inspired gadgets she hopes to forge from the tech we pilfered.

Anacaona pours another shot. She hasn't said a word since she got back from her expedition and showed us a video she recorded of herself wrecking the inside of one of the cryptobarons' condos with a sledge-hammer, laughing like a demon as she did it. I knew the spray-paint wouldn't be enough to sate her anger.

To get my sister talking, I pick one of the orange blossoms from a drooping flamboyán branch. Anacaona eyes me suspiciously as I tuck the flor into her hair. It's what our grandfather used to do, to remind her of her name's Taíno meaning.

"I don't want to talk about it," she says, nursing her cognac. "Not until it's confirmed."

Yuíza leans forward. "Until what's confirmed?"

"Ana," I say. "What did you see out there?"

"Nothing."

"Don't shut us out. Somos familia, remember?"

"I saw nothing. No sign of soldiers. No tanks. I think they're gone."

"The Chinese?"

Anacaona downs the cognac and refills her glass.

"The cold war went hot." Yuíza's dimples vanish in her grimace.

My heart is a drum beat in my chest. "This could be our chance."

Anacaona spits out her drink. "Are you loco?"

"Maybe a little," I chuckle.

"Vero has a point." Yuíza flicks her curls, a tic that means she is thinking. "Now could be our chance to take back the rest of the island. We have the numbers … for once."

"It's true!" Don Mateo shouts, clambering out of the workshop with Dagüao. "Our informers say there was a naval-wide order of mass retreat. Something big is happening on the mainland."

-Now is the time to strike.- I stand, mixing sign with speech. "To liberate Caguas, Guaynabo, Ponce, and Mayagüez."

Dagüao leans in. -Think of all we could make with the tech they left.-

Grinning like a comic book supervillain, Yuíza steeples her fingers.

Alcimar saunters into the nasa from the jungle, dropping a load of downed branches. "And what if you're wrong? What if it's a trap?"

I glance at him but he turns away, setting the blade of an ax into the thickest branch in the pile. "Don't you think it's worth the risk?" I scoff and am suddenly aware that my breath reeks of booze.

Alcimar leans against his axe, "And after the cities are 'free,' then what?"

The question frightens me, but I answer as best as I can. "We'll draft a constitution. Elect a government —"

"I thought we had everything we need." Alcimar approaches me. He rubs my back, hesitates before planting a kiss on my cheekbone. Between our raids of cryptocolonies, we've barely had the chance to talk through what we are to each other. But there is mutual affection and mutual respect. We are both learning how to open our hearts again.

He gets a good whiff of me and steps back. "Maybe we should revisit this tomorrow when you're not so … boracho."

"Good idea." Anacaona yawns. "I'm calling it a night. The rest of you dream up your fantasy tactics. I'm fine with whatever … as long as I get to use my sledgehammer."

"Macana," Yuíza says, correcting her. "I spent a lot of time making that thing, you have to call it by its proper name."

"Yeah, yeah," Anacaona says as she crosses to her bohio.

-Sleep?- Dagüao signs to Yuíza. She giggles and takes his hand as they leave the cancha together.

When I try to stand, my legs won't hold me. I grab at Alcimar. "I'm not drunk," I say, hearing the bleariness of my own words.

He frowns, but his eyes are laughing. He pats the hand that had latched onto his arm.

"Okay, maybe a little bit," I admit, my feet wobbling on what feels like unsteady ground.

He takes cognac straight from the bottle. Why doesn't he use a glass? Such a puerco.

"You know," he says, mouth pressed with feeling, "I'll follow you anywhere. But you have to remember you're asking them to go to war for you. Many of these jíbaros think like I used to. It's fine when you're a voice on the radio. It's another thing when you're there on the front-lines with them. To them, you'll never be Manuel Rojas."

I turn away from him. "After all our wins, how could they not trust me?"

Alcimar pulls me close, presses my head against his chest. He runs his fingers over my freshly buzzed hair. How did this brute end up so tender? "I just don't want to see you get hurt."

Our luck was going to run out eventually. We all knew that. But things had been going so well for so long I actually believed everything was going to be alright. I believed we could do anything, even take back our

Borikén. But this cacicazgo — this future without masters — was always just a dream.

Last month, we lost Alcimar. It still doesn't feel real. The drones left nothing to bury. So I wrapped his Yankees cap in white cloth, the way Abuela Serafina had done with her husband's body. We performed the itutu as best we could, burying what was left of him at the base of his favorite ceiba with a jar of the sweetest ñame we've harvested yet.

"May her roots reclaim the carpenter's son, may they carry him to the realm of the egun, where his family is waiting."

Doña Juana, a creyente, officiated the ceremony while I watched. Wax transformed into liquid, as fire transformed into smoke. Grandfather Abey called them opía, the spirits we would become after death. But Abey was not a creyente, his faith was not African or Iberian, he was a behike, devotee of the cemís, the dreaming stones that held up the sky.

I want to forget it all. But I have to remind myself of the price we paid for a freedom we could never win. Alcimar's screams on the radio haunt my dreams. The sound of proximity alarms. The thud of mechanical limbs. The Chinese were gone but their deadly sentinels were not. I sent my people marching to their deaths. And they'll never forgive me. Why should they?

Alcimar was right to doubt them, to doubt me. If the other yucayekes had stuck with our plan, we might have been alerted to the danger sooner. So few answered the call, and those that did had their own ideas about how to retake our cities. "Esa nena no sabe na," I overheard them say on one of the reserved frequencies. That's what they call me when my back is turned. "Nena." Little girl. Just like Mami and Papi.

Muchachita, you're confused. Get those gringo ideas out of your head. You shouldn't go back to university next semester. Stay here with your sisters. ¿Qué hiciste con mi niña? What have you done with my little girl? Oh almighty Señor, please forgive her for mutilating herself. Please forgive her, she is lost. If you are going to dress that way I don't want you in my house. You bring shame to this family. Vero▀▀▀ are you doing this to punish us?

When the shouting continued, Anacaona and Yuíza always rallied to my side. Father complained that he only had daughters, and yet refused to be blessed with a son. And our pure pastor Mami couldn't bear the rumors circulating around town that her child was becoming an "abomination." That was the word she used. The most I could get them to do was call me Vero. The nickname grandfather Abey used with me. His protest for not being allowed to name me after one of his long-vanished Taíno heroes. The fighting continued even as Teddy approached, Mami convinced the hurricane was the devil's work, that my life of sin had summoned it. In the end, Teddy had the last word. I climbed out of the wreckage just in time, my sisters following as they always did. And then came the wave of mud. *My deliverance.*

I regret not mourning them. I regret feeling relief when the burden of their implacable hatred and disappointment was washed away by brown waters. I felt nothing as Anacaona and Yuíza wept. My numbness was armor. I used it to remake our world. But now I am truly broken. I cry for Alcimar and the others killed trying to enact my vision. I cry because with each passing day our yucayeke is less a sanctuary and more a prison.

I wake to Don Brizuela's cuatro and Enriquillo's güiro. An unwelcome mañanita at an ungodly hour right outside my bohío. One of Puerto Rico's worst traditions, and not even Teddy could kill it.

"Estoy durmiendo," I protest, my voice raspy with unfinished dreams.

"Come on, hermanito!" That's Anacaona's artificially peppy voice.

"We need your help hauling these guineos!" Yuíza calls. "Doña Marta is going to make escabeche." Not the worst lie she could come up with. My stomach rumbles. Guineos en escabeche are sufficient motivation. Starchy sour deliciousness. I slip out of my bohío. The sun feels too warm and bright for morning.

Dagüao is the first face I see. He lifts his forearm to the sky, flicking his fingers repeatedly. -Good afternoon.-

I yawn. "Afternoon?"

I hear footsteps behind me, but before I turn around someone leaps onto my back. I manage to grab her legs in time.

"You can still catch me?"

"Of course." I lace my arms through Yuíza's legs. But I stagger, suddenly nauseous. The hangover has found me.

"How old are you again?" Anacaona tosses the guineos into a bin for Doña Marta.

"Okay people, the joy police have arrived." Yuíza scowls, dismounting her hungover steed.

"My turn!" Anacaona swoops in. She is much taller and heavier than Yuíza and I am on the verge of —

-No! He'll die,- Dagüao signs frantically.

But it is too late. We are all of us on the ground, a pile of giggling schoolchildren who have forgotten their age.

"Cacique!" A voice calls from down the mountain. "Cacique!"

Alonsito sprints through the trees, his umber skin slick with sweat. When he reaches the clearing, he rests his hands on his knees to catch his breath.

"Alonsito? ¿Qué te pasa?" Anacaona kneels, level with his frightened gaze.

"Aliens." He coughs between breaths. "Coming up the mountain. Pale like the chupacabra."

"The chupacabra is just a story, Alonsito," Yuíza says softly, in the voice of a former teacher's aide. "Sometimes our imagination —"

A shadow passes over the sun. I look up at a vast machine with a fluttering white sail. Its engine is barely audible as it passes over the valley. A dirigible of printed plastichrome. The airships of this new age of nanofabrics.

Alonsito clutches Anacaona's shirt as he points to something behind us. A trio of armored figures, faceless behind reflective visors and bone-white garb. The first of them strides forward, trailed by a shimmering orb with serrated plastichrome winglets and propellers. The ones behind stand perfectly still, their capes billowing in the mountain breeze.

"*Greetings, citizens.*" Their voice is a mechanically augmented, static-laced garble that reminds me of our early morning broadcasts to distant yucayekes.

I recoil at the word "citizen." Their uniforms display no golden stars on red flags. Not China then.

Alonsito hides in Anacaona's arms. "What do you want?" she asks, her voice firm.

"*We bring tidings from beyond these shores.*" Their hands move with inhuman grace. "*The treaty of Beijing has been signed. The war is over.*"

As Yuíza translates for Dagüao, her eyes are wide.

I give her a reassuring nod. "Guaitiao, you are our guest. But you haven't told us your name."

"*Our names are irrelevant. We are merely emissaries,*" they say. Are their suits designed to strip them of all affect? To dampen the humanity of their voices and their body language? Talk about cold diplomacy. "*We come to broker a peace, to offer you amnesty and salvation, to rebuild what was destroyed, should you elect to join us.*"

My eyes track the orb bobbing over the emissary's shoulder. "And who exactly is this *us*?"

"*A treaty was signed. An alliance was forged. To prevent global catastrophe, to end all wars, former adversaries have become one.*"

27

I wince at the strangeness of their speech. Surely this is the work of a real-time translator. With a gesture from their gloved hand, the spherical drone emits a cone of light. A Mercator projection of the globe, cast in a holographic translucency, ringed by white feathers.

"We are the United Nations Parliament."

Parliament. First it was a league, then a union, now, a parliament. An experiment in world governance intensifying with each successive global conflict. Rather than destroy each other, our enemies have fused, their empires merging in the name of peace and stability. Great.

Anacaona bursts into hysterical laughter. Laughter like a scream, like when she's trashing condos with a sledgehammer. A laughter you run from. Sensing the danger, Alonsito flings himself into Yuíza's arms.

"So you've come to take over China's lease?"

The emissary bows their head in supplication. *"You have but to ratify our accords and our riches will become your riches."*

They seek a paper conquest, I realize, my hands tightening into fists. Will this ever end?

Anacaona strikes the air. "Get out!"

"The unrest you have sown on this island has cost many lives." Their ghastly arms gesture to the clouds where one of their dirigibles is now hovering. *"Now you suffer needlessly. With our technology and resources, you could prosper. The choice is yours."*

If I hadn't pushed for the Reconquista of our cities, they would never have bothered to come here. They would have left us alone. Only now we pose a threat to their control and their image of peace and unity. *The choice is yours.* I hear my own words echoing back to me. I hear Alcimar arguing with me. Whispering in my ear as we make love. I hear him screaming on the radio as machines crush him. "You have a choice," I told them once, here in this cancha. *You have a choice.*

"We don't need your help," Anacaona snarls. "We outlived the Españoles, we outlived the Americanos, los Chinos, and we'll outlive you."

My sisters, my dear Dagüao, Don Mateo, Enriquillo, Doña Marta, Don Brizuela, and the others have gathered to hear what these "aliens" have to offer. In their desperate eyes, I see my failure. I remember Alcimar's cruel words. Words that now ring true even though he wouldn't have intended them to hurt in the end. *Stop pretending you're someone you're not.*

You have a choice.

"*Very well,*" the emissary says, and this time I can almost hear a glimmer of their humanity, a tiny flaw in the code. "*When you come to your senses, you will find the white minarets of our humanitarian consulates, our Missions, on the coast.*"

The emissary turns their back to us, but their voice carries through speakers somewhere in their suit. "*You have a choice.*"

The cacicazgo was always just a fantasy. A childish dream that an extinct civilization could be resurrected. A hope that ruin could be a pathway to renewal. A wish that the old ways could be revised to accommodate "abominations" like me. *Esa nena no sabe na.* To think that I could lead them. Anacaona is tougher than anyone I know. She never needed me. They would follow her. They might even thrive until the next La Niña cycle, when more Teddies would arrive.

"Wait," I say. The emissary halts mechanically. Everyone is watching me, but I cannot meet their eyes. "I'm coming with you."

Yuíza rushes to me, Dagüao close behind her. "What are you doing?" she whispers as she grips my shoulders.

Anacaona answers for me, her countenance strangely serene as she joins our circle. "He's doing what he needs to."

-Why leave us?- Dagüao signs, the unsteadiness of sorrow in his hands.

I bow my head in shame, make a circle on my chest with my clenched fist. -I'm sorry.-

-You are hurt,- Dagüao signs, saying what I can't.

29

I nod, unable to sign or speak.

"You'll come back?" Yuíza asks. In her voice I can hear the optimism cracking.

I want to reply yes, because I can't bear to hurt her, because I want to see that dimpled smile one last time before I disappear. But that would be dishonest. Rather than reply, I take her and Dagüao into my arms.

When I break the embrace, Anacaona stands solemnly before me. She speaks so that everyone can hear. She knows. She's taking the reins. "You've given so much to this community, Vero. But we haven't given you what you need. We hope you find what you're looking for out there."

We clutch each other tightly and she whispers in my ear, "Don't you dare forget us, cabrón."

I would laugh if I didn't feel so guilty. But I'm no good to them like this. I need to heal, and I can't do that here, in the place that has hurt me again and again.

"What will you do out there?" asks Don Mateo.

"I'll advocate for you, best I can," I say. "I'll share our stories."

That seems to satisfy some of them. Others are crying, whispering or signing rapidly. I wave one last time and then turn to the emissary who is as still as a statue.

I don't look back, not even as we soar over the cacicazgo. In their dirigible we sail the clouds to the coast, where I will accept their offer of amnesty for a life beyond these shores. A life where I can be who I am meant to be and chase the stories that I have always dreamed of telling.

"*What is your name?*" they ask me in their white halls.

"Vero," I tell them. A derivative of veritas. Latin for truth. Not as wondrous as the names divined by Yoruba Ifá or as glorious as those of the lost Caciques of the Taíno, but I like it because it is my own. I was always destined to be named Vero, but I get to decide what it means. My name. My truth. A descendant of slavers and those they enslaved;

their scars etched deep in my genes. A man born in the shape of a woman. A twin. My truth is paradoxes and contradictions. Hola. Hello. 你好. ‑Greetings.‑ Guaitiao.

In the pearly halls of their Mission, I tell Alonsito's aliens our truths. I tell them about a cacicazgo that dared to flourish in the abundant light and warmth of our star.

Excerpt from *Cacicazgo: How I Survived Hurricane Teddy*, A Memoir
by Vero Diaz

• •

desagüe | drought

"May the water be taken away, emptied out, so that the plate of the earth may be created — then may it be sown; then may dawn the sky and the earth. There can be no reverence given by what we have framed and what we have shaped, until humanity has been created."

Anonymous, *Popol Vuh*, circa 1550 CE

In the murk of the cistern, his quarry vaulted upward, shrieking. He found it amusing to think of the battered pail as prey caught within the well's mechanical jaws. He unhooked it from the pulley to set it in the dirt at his feet. The water reeked, a ferrous aroma not unlike blood. Signs of the contaminant. Reddish whorls that coiled like a storm.

Jodido.

Hydrophage. An indelible wound in the land that refused to heal.

Even the aquifer is scarred.

There in the prism of the tainted water, the old man's wizened visage undulated. Purple burns marbled his face like a mask, a constant reminder of calamity's reverb.

At least I'm alive.

Startled by what sounded like thunder, the old man nearly dropped the pail. A flock of sower drones crackled above him, trailing plumes of cyan mist in their wake as they lanced across the sky, over toppled stelae and sinking Maya ruins in the hills beyond. He tracked their avian shadows as their payloads descend in columns of vapor over the husks of trees that had once been lush chaparral. A green land scorched without flame.

Only the Caudillo could devise something crueler than burning.

He thought of the landscape as parched bones, the drones as necromancers attempting resurrection. With the flock receding on the horizon, the man resumed his work, hauling his spoils up the slope to the Casa Sórdida, or Centro de Refugiados, as the United Nations Parliament had designated the encampment. During the war, he was told that this path was a key supply route for the guerillas opposing the Caudillo's regime. The Lobos. He had heard many stories, but he could not remember as others could. Imagination would have to suffice.

He tried not to splash water as he ascended. Though spry for a septuagenarian, Abuelo, as his fellow sórdidos called him, could not remember the war or much that preceded it. While some had lost memories due to trauma at the hands of the Caudillo's death squads, Abuelo's lapses were of an entirely different nature.

Like many of his generation, Abuelo was a victim of the Androvirus, carrying the disease asymptomatically for decades, only to lose his episodic memories in a matter of months as amyloid plaques occluded his neural pathways. That old saying was true: ignorance was bliss. God had gifted him the affliction as an act of mercy.

The Casa loomed ahead, the stolid faces of the sórdidos peering out from the slits in the concrete that served as windows. They watched him with vague interest, bodies slouched, bereft of vitality. He often wondered if they envied him, if they longed to forget as he had.

33

A sweat droplet coasted down his forearm, teasing him to itch the spot where his bar-code was still visible. He could not remember being tagged in the labor camps. He could not even remember the faces of his kin or his own name, but he was alive, and that had been enough to keep him going.

The Casa Sórdida was a refuge built from the debris of a demolished barracks. Once-blue tarps were strewn across the concrete foundations. Corrugated steel roofs cross-hatched pockets of open sky. These disparate elements of rubble were buttressed into something habitable by donations from the United Nations Parliament and what little the new "People's Government" could spare. Here they housed the forgotten ones, los sórdidos. Casualties of war that still drew breath. Refugees persevering at the edge of oblivion.

At least I don't remember.

Abuelo strode into the sala where Doña Margarita was frying something in amber oil. She fished fritters from the oil, setting them to cool on a cutting board beside a bushel of green plantains — a gift from the UN's Mission in the Green Zone. He set the water on her countertop.

"Rojo? Again?" Doña Margarita sighed as she examined the fouled contents of the bucket. She flicked clumps of dough from her huipil, the most colorful in her collection of handwoven garments. "We'll have to use two neutralizer packets today. With the grace of God, there will be enough to hold us until the next shipment comes."

Abuelo shrugged. "Lo siento." Disappointing Doña Margarita was something he hated to do, especially since she cooked for him.

"Never mind. Go get comfortable, la comida ya está listo," she said, her russet cheeks creasing into a smile as she loaded a ceramic tray with crispy molotes. A rare treat. "After all, it is your birthday."

With a good-natured grumble, Abuelo meandered to the mottled leather sofa. He slumped beside José Antonio, who muttered to himself. This was not unusual. When he was lucid, José Antonio was

34

Abuelo's best source for information about the war, and his only friend in this austere place. It was in moments like these — when José Antonio's sepia face was contorted as he relieved the violence of the war — that Abuelo envied him most.

"Primo, if only you had been there to see it," he said, staring at the soft green husks of the peeled plantains on the counter. "The trees, the fields, all of it shriveled in an instant."

Abuelo steepled his fingers, recalling the storm of rust in the pail. "Hydrophage."

"For generations, we kept this land green." José Antonio clutched Abuelo's forearm. "And then ... one day — poof. Gone. Can you imagine it?"

Abuelo tried to imagine as José Antonio did, but he couldn't.

José Antonio nodded. "You know, I met him once, the rebel leader."

"Hector Beltrán Rosa?"

José Antonio was smiling now, clearly proud to have known someone of influence. "He told us that revolutionaries are sowers."

Abuelo could feel José Antonio's hand quivering now, the sweat of the man's palm slick against his skin. "He never got to see his seeds sprout. The Caudillo's macheteros saw to it that he didn't. Him and his family met their end in fire, just like —" José Antonio trailed off, his eyes tearful.

"Your family?" Abuelo asked, knowing the answer, wishing he didn't. The sobbing usually began at this point, when José Antonio would recount how he was forced to watch his family murdered, before being shipped off to Quetzal, the labor camp.

Rebellion has a price.

"Felíz cumpleaños!" Doña Margarita handed Abuelo a plate of crispy molotes and coffee in a tin mug left behind by the soldiers that once mustered here.

He nodded in thanks before devouring the moist and delicately crisped fritters, an upgrade from the bioprinted proteins they had been subsisting on in a land where little grew.

"Enjoy," Doña Margarita said with a smile as she heaped more fritters onto his plate. Even then, behind the mask of her smile, he could see that glimmer of sadness, that faint echo of horror animating her amber eyes. She was of them too. Broken and yearning. Sórdida. What cruel fate brought her here? He preferred not to know.

With false teeth he chewed the starchy molotes, rallying the humor to thank the Caudillo for branding his date of birth on his skin. If not for this now-forgotten violence, he would not remember his own birthday and would have no excuse for celebration. Between mouthfuls of plantain, he swallowed one of the pink pills he kept in a crumpled ziplock bag in his pocket. This was the medicine that halted the progression of the Androvirus, the only thing keeping him from forgetting what happened yesterday and the day before that. One of many miracles provided by the UN's new Mission in the Green Zone.

"And for you, joven?" Doña Margarita gestured to an unfamiliar young woman seated on a broken stool at the edge of the sala.

The stranger did not carry herself like a sórdida. Even though he had never seen her before, some ghost of familiarity lurked in the sharp blade of her jaw or the total blackness of her eyes.

Joven.

While robbed of his episodic memory, Abuelo retained some residual *feeling* for the past. His body remembered things. His physique, unhampered by arthritis or an overly bent posture, did not resemble that of a laborer or campesino in the twilight of his life. Strangely, though, Abuelo was adept with a shovel, among the best in the team sent to dig the new foundation for the recently constructed annex. José Antonio once joked that before the war he was likely a personal trainer with an "eye for ergonomics" sent to the labor camps by the Caudillo to fix "everyone's bad form." The joke comforted as much as it troubled him. His body was a vessel of living history, its contents irretrievable. But now something about this woman, this outsider, stirred up the past from its dormant seat in his guts.

"Nothing, gracias." She nodded deferentially to Doña Margarita, the deep resonance of her voice almost startling. "I've already eaten."

Doña Margarita grumbled with disappointment. "Café? Algo para tomar?"

The young woman rose from her chair, tilting her head toward Abuelo. "I've come to take a walk with that one."

He glanced warily at Doña Margarita, who had become something of a confidante to him and many in Casa Sórdida. She nodded in approval, clearly pleased that someone had taken an interest in one of her lonely charges. He gulped his coffee down to the charred dregs of cinnamon at the bottom, before stepping outside with the stranger.

"You can call me Aleja." She offered a velvety hand, shaking his arm with surprising vigor. "I've come to help you."

He searched her face for a resemblance to his own. Her skin was a deep copper tone, far darker than his pinkish tan, her nose was not aquiline as his was, and her hair was perfectly straight. She had what people called "the look of an india." Despite the differences in their appearance, Abuelo ventured a guess. "Are you familia?"

"No," Aleja said, lacing her arm through his. They strode past the shanty of zinc-roofed shacks and makeshift concrete structures that abutted the Casa and headed into the desert. "But I may be able to help you remember them."

On the dusty footpath, they weaved through corridors of hydrophage-corroded brush, petrified carcasses of mesquite now encrusted with pale fungal blooms.

"They're calling it Artificial Sapience," Aleja said. "A team of scientists with the United Nations Parliament have built a quantum supercomputer powerful enough to overcome Moore's Law. They're using it to conduct research. Simulations. Experiments. They believe it might cure Androvirus."

Abuelo frowned, pulling his bag of pills from his pocket. "But we already have a cure."

"Antivirals only halt the progression of the disease. Our vaccines inoculate against *future* infections. Neither can restore that which has been lost," Aleja said, veering east at a fork in the sooty trail.

Abuelo followed her lead. He searched the petrified ranks of palms, gum trees, and ceibas for a memory of what they looked like before the hydrophage. He imagined them screaming when the hydrophage detonated. He'd read somewhere that plants could scream.

"With Sapience, we may be able to reverse the damage to your memory."

Abuelo halted partly to catch his breath, partly to process her claim. "How is this possible?"

"The treatment is experimental. It starts with medicine that breaks up amyloid plaques in the hippocampus and elsewhere in your brain. Then we use cognitive behavioral therapy to promote memory retrieval. Artificial Sapience will use a combination of machine learning, targeted neurogenesis, and epigenomic sequencing to direct our progress and heal your mind."

They continued up the chalky path, Aleja providing support to her elder as they ascended.

"Hippocampus," Abuelo grunted as he climbed the path. "The memory center of the brain."

"How often does it happen?" Aleja asked. In the setting sun, the thick layers of her makeup were visible.

"How often does what happen?"

"Those moments when you remember?"

"Once or twice a day." Abuelo surveyed the treeless hills that ringed the valley, trying to imagine the wildlife that once lived there. "My bones remember what my mind cannot." But his mind did remember some things. *Roses that scream when cut. Roald Dahl. Sound*

Machine. 1949.

"When I was a little girl, all of this was more colorful than you can possibly imagine. But I want you to try," Aleja said. "See the deep green of the ceiba canopies. See the gold of the flowering hibiscus, the white of xtabentun blossoms. See the cotingas, their wings in flight, feathers bright as suns." Aleja combed her fingers through what used to be a palm frond hanging over the path. It now resembled some kind of ashen sculpture, dendritic talons reaching.

Did it scream when it died?

She gestured to the arboreal sepulcher around them. "Imagine the air thick with the breath of the forest, saguaros vaulting through the trees after dusk, howling."

"I see nothing when I close my eyes but ..."

Saguaros. Also known as Howler Monkeys. In myth, they —

"Someone told me they were people once," Abuelo ventured.

"A myth of the Maya," Aleja replied, still transfixed by the petrified palm. "They are what remains of a version of humanity shaped from wood."

In the long curve of its branches, Abuelo imagined the missing simians. Vestiges of a distant age, like his sórdidos. "What happened to the rest of these wooden people?"

Aleja smirked. "They were punished by the gods for their vanity. Drowned in a great flood."

The gods. Chaak. Fangs carved in stone. K'uk'ulkan. Feathered serpent coiling on a smudged fresco. Ix Chel. Goddess emptying a water jar. Madrid Codex. Page 74.

"A sad story," Abuelo said, the sharp ink lines of remembered Maya glyphs still vivid in his mind.

We could use one of those floods right now.

"So —" Aleja cleared her throat. "Can I count you in?"

"Joven, of course, but you should know that I have nothing." Abuelo reached into a pocket as if to confirm his destitution. "I have no way to pay for this."

Aleja continued down the track into the valley. "Since the treatment is experimental, there is no cost. We only ask for your cooperation."

"We?"

"I'm with the Peoples' Government. Information Ministry," Aleja said. "You can think of me as an Archivist. My task is to recover the past, what little the Caudillo left of it, so that we might build a better tomorrow and stop another like him from rising again."

They arrived at a roadblock, boulders arrayed in a rectangular formation. He had seen this kind of structure before. Aleja beckoned him to sit with her in the middle of the dusty court of stones. They rested in silence, looking out over the valley, an expanse of greyish-brown broken only by spheres of nano-printed plastichrome to the south, where the UN Parliamentarians had created microclimates stable enough to resume agriculture and address the famine. Aleja's attention, however, was not drawn to the Green Zone but the ground beneath their feet. With a petrified twig she etched something into the loess.

"The Caudillo knew that the only way to preserve his rule was to obliterate the past, to make the present eternal." Following her precise strokes, Abuelo watched a sequence of numbers appear in the dirt. "It began with the severing of the optical network, the burning of paper records, the demolition of cloud facilities and hard disks. He incinerated all traces of his victims. The cadavers and their digital ghosts."

She grabbed a fistful of red earth, scattering it over her industry, reducing the numbers to memory.

Prisoner 10290-889-492942-1.

"Those numbers … I recognize them." Abuelo tapped the barcode on his left forearm. "You've come for *me* specifically."

Aleja nodded. "If the dream of every tyrant is to reduce the world to an unending present with no past or future, then it is the job of those who resist to ensure that some skeletons remain for posterity." She studied him with a strained expression, then climbed to her feet. Perhaps she found his burns revolting.

"Someone did resist," she said, dusting off her pants. "Someone working within the regime." She pointed to the wan hills to the south-west, to a heap of pale stones. Pillars. Stelae. Staircases. The remains of a Maya temple complex, shrouded in wafting dust.

"Beneath the Maya ruins lies a bunker, part of a vast subterranean network. It was built to remember those the Caudillo sought to erase. Bits of them reside there in half-burnt files, rusting hard disks, molding ID cards and photographs."

Abuelo folded his arms, taking note of recurring motifs in the temple's architecture: a fanged deity with an elongated nose, stony crests in the shape of a cross without its head.

Chaak, Lord of Rain — 89.726573.

He wiped sweat from his brow. The memories both encouraged and frightened him. "What does this have to do with me?"

"Your bar-code is indexed." Aleja helped him to his feet. Her hands were markedly coarse and weathered for someone so young. "In a high-priority database. Your five-digit prefix marks you as one of the Caudillo's most wanted. Just as the war was ending, they issued a mass execution order for anyone with this prefix." Aleja's hair shimmered in the waning sunlight; something about it seemed too perfect.

What could he have done to become so infamous to the Caudillo? Abuelo suppressed tremors of excitement.

"We need to find out what you knew." Aleja studied his quivering body as if it were a hidden language. "We need to know why you were so dangerous to the regime." Her voice softened with pain. "We've lost so many." Behind those black irises, he could feel relived horrors surg-ing, perhaps triggered by talk of the war. But when he searched inside himself for flickers of that dark chapter, he found and felt nothing. Was it better to forget, to remain oblivious? Was it better to live in this eternal present, or to remember as she did?

Who did you lose, joven?

"There's more. It won't be easy to hear. But you have the right to know what we have come to suspect — why we need your help. Our intelligence operatives have evidence that a rogue cell of militants loyal to the Caudillo is operating underground. We suspect that they're in the midst of planning an attack — that they mean to avenge his death, perhaps reinstall one of his surviving lieutenants as leader and undo all that the People's Government and the UN Parliament have worked so hard to rebuild."

Abuelo froze mid-stride. The cycle of war was renewing.

Buluc Chabtan will be pleased. Let the rivers run red. Let his thirst be slaked. Let the weak be culled —

"You're serious?" Abuelo rasped.

"There may be a weapons cache hidden somewhere in the countryside. Invisible to our scanners, but known by someone within the regime or one of our lost spies."

"And that's who you think I am?"

"Possibly," she said, avoiding his hungry gaze. They turned back towards the Casa as the sun dipped beneath the mountain ridge, casting a sanguine pall over the land. His red world. A world of beauty and bloodshed. A poisoned world. A world of swirling rust in battered pails. A desert world that yearned to be lush. Abuelo also yearned. He wanted to remember the chatter of monkeys. The whisper of leaves.

"I'll do it, but you must help me find my family or whoever might be looking for me."

Aleja shook her head. "Our facial recognition tech is not turning up anything on your identity. The burn damage to your face may be too extensive, or the records were destroyed. I can't tell you who you were, but perhaps through this treatment, you can answer that for yourself."

He focused on her eyes, yearning to see that glimmer of vibrant memory that he did not possess. "I don't want to be a sórdido anymore. Living like this isn't living at all."

As he spoke, Abuelo looked to the reddening sky, as if appealing directly to his Creator. His hand found Aleja's and he squeezed it with trembling fingers. "Is it vain to think God spared my life for some grander purpose?"

Aleja gently removed herself from his grip. "If this procedure works, you could be the first person to beat this disease. Think of the others who could be saved if we're successful. If that isn't divine purpose, I don't know what is."

Inside the Casa, Abuelo passed through the open-air kitchen, his appetite tickled by the lingering fragrance of molotes. A feast made in his honor. He smiled at the memory, and so many others like it, of him and the others sharing food, of Doña Margarita's care for them. Perhaps this could be a foundation on which to build a new life if nothing came of Aleja's procedure. He couldn't get his hopes up for anything more.

Gathered in pairs or trios along the barren walls, the sórdidos stared at him as he made his way to their new dormitory in the annex. It was rare to see them so animated. Most days he thought of them as a horde of undead. Swaying in place, they relived past traumas instead of inhabiting this hellish present. Some of the women dressed like Doña Margarita, their huipiles a smattering of color and geometry. The sórdidos consisted of displaced Tzeltal and Tzotzil peoples from the highlands of the former state of Chiapas, uprooted Lacandones, the forest caretakers, and Yucatec-speaking Maya from the coast, conscripted to fight when the borders were shuttered and the tourists stopped coming. Then there were the Ladinos, peasants of mixed ancestry like José Antonio, who lost everything in the war. Perhaps the sórdidos were envious of his outing with the stranger from elsewhere.

He proceeded to the dormitory, where bedding was heaped on the cement floor in rows and columns. He claimed his usual pile at the far edge by the window. José Antonio was awake, sitting upright. On some nights, José Antonio would wait up for him, hoping to play cards, reminisce about his life, or on rare occasions when the others were fast asleep, seek the comfort of his touch. These days, Abuelo struggled to be good company, his mind preoccupied.

"What did she want?" José Antonio asked. Outside, dusk seeped through the iron bars girding the window, dappling his face with rosy light.

Abuelo laid out his bedding and sat down beside him. "Do you ever wish you could forget?

Curling into fetal position, José Antonio pulled the covers over his head. "Who would I be if I forgot?"

Abuelo couldn't sleep. Instead, he studied a pale stain on the wall, a milky archipelago seeping from a gap in their makeshift ceiling. The sun's scorching rays had bleached the aging paint over many cloudless days. With a coat of fresh paint, it could be fixed.

A week had passed since Aleja's visit, and every day since had felt like an eternity. Walking was the only medicine. Walking to the well. Walking along the trails. Walking to the ruins. Before Aleja, Abuelo had been content to live out his days, yearning for what might have been, but content, nonetheless, with being alive. On the dimmest days, he had Doña Margarita's cooking to look forward to, but even that simple joy had become less satisfying. Since Aleja, his squalid circumstances felt intolerable. He was overcome with a new yearning. A desire burned in him. A voice in his head, that other self that rattled the cage of his afflicted mind.

Get me out of here.

He made another loop behind the Casa, where the corpses of magueys abutted the dusty trail. The possibility that Aleja's visit had been a grand deception, or even worse, a fantasy of his Androvirus-addled brain, contributed to his growing sense of dread.

"Abuelito, where are you off to?"

Abuelo looked up to see Ismael, one of the Casa's few youths, a young man with rare energy. "I have to maintain this boyish figure," he said with a smile, turning to find Ximena jogging to catch up. Like Ismael, Ximena had been orphaned by the war. To be raised in this hell was not a fate Abuelo would wish on anyone, but the two of them seemed balanced enough.

He adjusted his sombrero, squinting through the bright sun.

Ismael stopped just short of him, a quizzical look playing on his lips. "You look like you could use some company." His jet-black hair, like Ximena's, fell past his shoulders.

Abuelo thumbed his chin. "Doña Margarita put you up to this?"

Ximena looked away, laughing.

"Of course not!" Ismael threw an arm around Abuelo's shoulder.

Since Aleja's now infamous visit, the pair had shown an unusual interest in Abuelo's well-being. Abuelo entertained them, their joy a welcome distraction from his obsessive thoughts. He steered them along the path behind the Casa, passing through a plot of land dotted with wooden crosses: the refuge's humble cemetery and, further down the path, the makeshift flower beds that Doña Margarita dreamed might someday be a garden.

"If you find out you're rich, don't forget about us," Ismael said.

"If I am, my gift to you will be a ring," Abuelo replied. He allowed the silence to thicken before peering over at Ximena, who'd already cracked a smile. "So that you can get on with it already."

"Perdón?" Ismael asked, feigning confusion.

"I may not remember anything," Abuelo kicked at the dust with the worn tip of his boot, "but I have two good eyes, and you two aren't fooling anyone."

Ximena clasped Abuelo's arm. She was maybe eighteen, but with her dark hair tucked into a bun, she looked older. She turned to Ismael. "Don't worry, I'm patient," she whispered, just loud enough for Abuelo to hear.

He hoped his smile looked genuine. "Most of us have forgotten there is more to life than our suffering. What you have gives us hope … and something to gossip about."

Ismael patted Abuelo on the back. "Glad to be a source of entertainment."

"Perhaps you're too young," Abuelo said, his voice low as they stepped past the ivory-hued husks of ceibas. "But what do you recall of what it was like before the hydrophage?"

"I remember the smell of rain," Ximena spoke slowly. "The sound of it dripping from one leaf to the next through the canopy."

"I confuse dreams for memories," Ismael said as he edged closer to Ximena. "I remember birds. I used to try to catch them when I was little. So many colors. Like Doña Margarita's huipil."

Abuelo savored their descriptions, probing his memory for a trace of the world they described. In that moment, he felt as if these two youths, with their stories of bygone days, were his elders.

When they arrived at the entrance to the Casa, Ximena stopped mid-stride, her gaze drawn to a crowd pouring from the sala. "What's all the commotion?"

"It must be Aleja," Abuelo stammered, his pace quickening. "She's come back —"

Ismael spoke over him. "If this whole thing goes nowhere, I want you to know that you always have us. No matter who you were, you'll always be our abuelo. Even if you aren't a millionaire."

Inside the Casa, he found Doña Margarita sitting across from a slender man in a stylish grey suit and tie. The man's face was bronzed and boyish, his wiry black hair tightly-cropped, with a few white flecks that read like battle scars. Over his shoulder a spherical drone whirred, tracking the man's exuberant hand gestures. Abuelo held his breath, sensing that he was interrupting something important. The man had the polished, resonant tenor of a television personality and his Spanish was musical. Abuelo recognized the accent as Caribbean, with its clipped consonants, rounded vowels, and the "l" that sometimes replaced the "r" at the end of words.

"Let me get this straight — you're telling me you aren't employed by the United Nations or the People's Government. That you are here of your own accord to take care of these people?"

"This is my home."

"But you're not like the others, you could lead a fulfilling life in the city."

"There's nothing out there that I can't have here." A hint of frustration crept into Doña Margarita's voice. "This is where I choose to be. These people are my family now."

The man seemed disarmed by Margarita's conviction. He sat back in his seat, contemplating her further. "Thank you for sharing your story with me, Doña. I think a lot of people will find what you're doing here inspiring."

"I wouldn't know." Margarita shrugged and fled to her familiar post in the kitchen, busying herself with a shipment of maize from the Green Zone. "But if there are others you wish to speak to, I only ask that you be respectful."

"Doña," the man called, getting up from the sofa, trailed by the drone. "Our experiences may be different, but in my country, many too have suffered." He rolled up his sleeves and joined Margarita behind the counter. "We know what it's like to be left with nothing and still make the most of it."

Margarita demonstrated how to properly peel the maize. Abuelo could tell by the vigor of her peeling that she was pleased the man took an interest in her work. "So this place makes you feel nostalgic?"

"Nostalgia is a good word for it." The man tugged at an ear of corn, struggling with a particularly tough husk. Margarita took the corn from him, submerging it in a bin of tepid water. "Many of us are ruled by our pasts. Running to what is familiar, running away from what hurts us. I guess that's why I'm so intrigued by this place, its story. It reminds me ..."

Margarita piled the peeled maize in a bin. Abuelo hoped she might use it for tamales. As if she could hear his grumbling stomach, she looked up from her corn husks, and waved for him to enter. The man approached from the countertop, his drone whirring behind him. "And who is this caballero?"

"Nobody," Abuelo said as he slumped into the sofa cushions, craning his neck to look around the room. No Aleja.

"No one is nobody," the man persisted.

"I was someone once," Abuelo sighed. "But not anymore." He didn't want to talk to anyone but Aleja.

"Vero Diaz." The man leaned forward to offer his hand. "I'm a reporter with the *Daily Harbinger*," he said, as if his news outlet needed no introduction. Abuelo did not recognize the name.

"I'm afraid I can't be of much help to you."

"He has Andro," Margarita said from behind them, over the clatter of dishes. "But the government is helping him. They bring meds with the shipments."

Vero's eyes widened with interest. "You remember nothing of the war?"

"Nothing at all." Abuelo shifted in his seat. "But sometimes, I feel things when people talk about the past. Some part of me remembers. But not my mind … not yet."

"Fascinating." Vero signaled for the drone to zoom in. "Would you mind going on the record for an article about the Centro de Refugiados?"

"What are we without memories?" Abuelo replied with a nod. What did it matter? If Aleja wasn't coming this might be his only chance. If the article spread widely maybe someone would recognize him. As he spoke, the drone circled them. "I have none of your 'nostalgia.' I share none of their trauma." He lifted his chin to the sórdidos clustered around the salon's largest window, peering in at their interview. "I am simply here, day in and day out. Like a circle, I have no beginning."

Vero appraised him as he spoke. Abuelo felt his gaze on the burns and the scars. "Perhaps *this* is your story. This place. These people."

Abuelo grunted a dismissal. "Earlier you said that our Casa was familiar." He spread his arms wide in a gesture toward their humble surroundings. "What did you mean by that?"

Vero tugged at the collar of his pressed shirt. "I was there in Puerto Rico when Teddy hit."

Abuelo nodded, which Vero took as a cue to continue.

"We were on our own. Had very little, like you." Vero rubbed his hands together. "But it was different."

"How?"

"We were family."

That stopped Margarita in her tracks. Abuelo half expected her to abandon her kitchen to correct this reporter. It wasn't so different. Without the sórdidos, Doña Margarita would be lost.

Vero waved a hand dismissively. "That chapter of my life is over. I can't forget like you can — not in the same way. But I have moved on."

Abuelo laughed bitterly. "Then why have you come here to this familiar place?"

"I don't need to explain myself to you." Vero's hands clenched into fists and Abuelo secretly congratulated himself for getting a rise out of him. "This is a story that needs telling. Lately, all you hear about on the feeds are the UN's latest techno miracle. No one is paying attention to people like you —"

Abuelo shushed Vero with a frantic wave of his hand.

"What is it?"

As Vero spoke, Margarita had moved to the hallway to greet someone. Abuelo strained to hear the conversation, but Doña Margarita's voice overwhelmed the softer words of the visitor. "Why of course, joven — he's just over here in the sala."

Joven. At the word, Abuelo's heart swelled.

Margarita rushed into the room, Aleja trailing behind her at a casual pace. Vero stood up to greet the newcomer. Her deep brown complexion was reddened by the afternoon sun or foundation a shade too ruddy.

Vero regarded the outsider, whose worn fatigues and threadbare vest made her look like a guerilla. "Could I get your name? I'm documenting —" Vero's drone spun around to center Aleja in its frame, but Abuelo stood, blocking the machine's line of sight.

"Aleja!" Abuelo rushed toward her. "I never doubted you. I knew you would come. I knew —"

"I was delayed unexpectedly." Aleja patted the old man's shoulder. "My apologies."

Margarita smiled. "Won't you stay for dinner? I'm making fresh tamales de chipilín." She pointed to a plastic cola bottle hanging on a hook over the sink where greens coiled up from a bed of soil. "I grew the herbs myself."

"You are so generous," Aleja said. "But Abuelo and I have much to discuss."

Three months into the treatment, Abuelo started to have what Aleja insisted were flashbacks. Some were triggered by regressive therapy sessions. Others appeared in his drug-induced dreams, gripping him with vivid, haunting sensations and images. The smell of smoke. People writhing in flames. Screams interrupted by gunfire.

Abuelo had little doubt that these were echoes of the violence that webbed his face with burns. And then there was that voice, that shadow of his past self that increasingly crept into his thoughts.

That afternoon, Abuelo met Aleja in the usual spot, the strange court of monoliths where she had etched his barcode in silt. She waved to him, a long wooden box set on the ground by her feet.

"How are you feeling today, Abuelo? Are we any closer to a name today?"

Shaking his head, Abuelo removed his straw sombrero. "None of the names on the recording sparked anything. Will we be trying foreign names too?"

"Not today, but I'll cycle those in over time." She gestured to the box at her feet. "Open it."

As he approached the container, Abuelo searched her face for any sign for what it might contain, but her look betrayed nothing. The rusty handle groaned as he pulled it.

"We are transitioning to the final phase of your treatment." Aleja's voice softened as he reached inside.

Why are you nervous?

"In the next few weeks, the pace of your memory reclamation will accelerate. It may bring you discomfort."

Abuelo lurched backward upon recognition of the object. A standard-issue QBZ-30. The preferred smart-carbine of the Chinese infantry, wielded on the battlefields of the Sino-American war. Something burned inside him, something shapeless and horrific. He staggered and fell to one knee, breathing hard.

"Get up!" Aleja said, her severity startling him.

He obeyed, approaching the weapon warily.

"Take it."

As if her words were an order or an incantation, he found himself reaching into the box, lifting the frame of the firearm. A first generation of plastichrome, the printed weapon still had a bit of weight.

"Load the rifle."

Startled by how fluid his movements were, Abuelo snapped the ultra-thin magazine into place. He rested the edge of the weapon against the groove of his shoulder, anticipating recoil.

Abuelo gasped. "I've done this before."

Aleja wasn't listening. She was crouched in the court stones, tending to something in the ground. *White smoke.* Her face flickered, tinged crimson as flames leapt from the controlled blaze at her feet. The odor overwhelmed him. Not the sweetness of wood. Not the acridness of gasoline. It was something primal that elicited a flicker of recall, a sickly flutter in Abuelo's pulse.

Flames unremitting. Bodies charred in white-hot smolder. The reverberations of gunshots. Air vibrating, screaming.

Abuelo howled at the memory until his voice rasped with terror. Over the ringing in his ears he could barely hear Aleja's voice calling him back to the present. What had he seen in that flash of a moment? A girl bathed in blood — no, engulfed in flame. Her eyes pleading with him. He could look away from her but the others — the wolf-men — were coming.

Gripped by the past's red currents, Abuelo tried to pull away but his body moved of its own accord. He closed his eyes, afraid of what he would find in the dark of his mind. He focused on the woman's voice. The one calling to him. He anchored himself to her resonance. But the girl was still there. Screaming.

I'll save you.

His finger hovered over the trigger, his carbine aimed at the siren luring him.

I'll deliver you.

Then the release. A sweet fury of sparks and molten metal. A symphony of violence.

Liberate me.

The firearm fell to his feet, released from his iron grip. He covered his head with his forearms, trying to shield himself from the roar of gunfire, the screams — echoes of that other life. Abuelo shut his eyes, too afraid to look at what this fugue wrought. He could still feel the carbine's residual heat in the air, on his hands. How could he have done this? He had killed Aleja, the woman who had helped him, the woman who had become his friend.

Now I'll never remember.

"I'm alright!"

Aleja's hand was on his shoulder, shaking him until his eyes regained focus. She was unharmed.

"It's a smart-gun! I pre-programmed the ballistic trajectory to avoid living targets."

Still panting, Abuelo stood on legs trembling with adrenaline. "That's not funny, joven." He'd shot her — he would have killed her. What memory could compel such an action?

"You were frightened," Aleja said gently. "What you did was not an uncommon response to trauma."

"You could have warned me."

Aleja folded her arms, the warmth evaporating from her voice. "I thought you were serious about remembering."

Abuelo grumbled affirmatively. Her tactics were questionable, but they were working.

A tickle in his throat turned into a cough and he tasted smoke on his tongue. "What was that smell?"

"Human hair." She gestured to the charred remnants of the fire at her feet. "The smell of your hair burning must have been traumatic. I thought this might bring what happened to the surface. Was I right?"

Wolf-men. Painted red.

"I remember a fire," Abuelo said, war paint sticky in his mind. "The Lobos were there. I was with them."

Aleja studied his expression for things left unsaid.

"And there was a girl," Abuelo panted. "She died."

The woman squinted at him and locked the carbine inside its case. "I think that's all for today."

Their pace back through the fossilized copse was brisker than usual and Abuelo could feel a new urgency swirling around Aleja. As they passed a sunken Maya temple, he hummed a melody he did not recognize. Abuelo sipped from his flask, staring at the ruins. "Has anyone excavated that one?"

"Not yet," Aleja answered. "We have other priorities. And it's dangerous."

"Dangerous?"

"In Palenque," Aleja said, "archaeologists found a tomb. When they unsealed the sarcophagus within, they found a body smothered in cinnabar, a highly toxic substance, prized by the Maya for its brilliant color."

A crimson skeleton. A mask of buffed malachite.

"The Red Queen," Abuelo replied, surprised by the memory.

"The past can be dangerous."

54

When they reached the doorway to the Casa where he could smell Doña Margarita's frijoles, Aleja grabbed his shoulder, turned him to face her. "The Caudillo used fire to punish only the most reviled of his enemies. We're getting closer." Her eyes shimmered, inky mascara like wet charcoal.

"This is personal, isn't it?"

"War always is," she said. "Perhaps when we're through here I can tell you my story."

"You were one of the Lobos, weren't you?" he said, peering into the black of her eyes.

"Most of us in the People's government were," Aleja said, in that half-answering tone he had become accustomed to. "But if you want to know, I was there — a child at the height of it. And now, as we rebuild, I refuse to allow anyone to forget what they did to us, what we had to become to stop the regime."

"Fire with fire," Abuelo whispered, his hand tracing the rubbery grafts of skin where he'd once had hair. "I was told the Lobos used fire to execute the Caudillo."

"Yes, it was revenge for what he did to our Commander, Hector Beltrán Rosa." Aleja lowered her gaze. "That was a difficult day."

Abuelo thought of the sunken temple. "The Maya used fire to commune with their Gods."

Dresden codex. Page 39. A canid holding torches — 89.726573.

"The Caudillo wanted to play God," Aleja scoffed. "But I suppose that's what we're doing with this treatment." She opened the heavy door to the Casa for him. "I've upped the dose of your meds. Are you ready?"

Abuelo nodded, but as she turned to leave, he held her arm. "The temple, the one that you showed me —"

"What about it?"

With Aleja's arm still in his grasp, Abuelo was comforted by the leathery feel of her skin. Skin like his. "I can tell by the architectural style that it's from the post-Classic period. Built just before the Spaniards arrived in the Yucatán."

Aleja clapped with delight. "So you *are* ready!"

Despite their breakthrough, the next sessions were not as fruitful as either Abuelo or Aleja had hoped for. They were no closer to determining his name, but more details about his upbringing had become clear. They were certain Abuelo had been raised in an affluent family, that he had university training as an archaeologist, though none of the professorate who could have corroborated his credentials had survived the Caudillo's purge of the intelligentsia. At some point he had joined the Lobos' rebellion, which explained his extensive military training and the fiery visions that haunted him.

Abuelo untethered the rusty pail from the pulley system, marveling at the crystal clarity of the water it contained. A week prior, UN peacekeepers had brought specialized pneumatic drones from the Green Zone. They looked like angels in their all-white garb as they drilled into the aquifer, injecting the neutralizer agent directly into the bedrock. This made Abuelo's once disheartening chore of fetching water from the well a more hopeful errand. As he turned to leave, he studied the stonework along the well. He suspected this aquifer was one node in an ancient network of cenotes engineered by the Maya to irrigate their crops and cities.

If the land can heal, so can I.

With the water in hand, he ascended the hill to the Casa whistling as he went, returning to the tune he had first recalled after he'd nearly shot Aleja in the stone court. A simple repeating pattern. It flowed from his lips with ease.

89.726573.

José Antonio, who rarely ventured out of the Casa, was strolling down the path toward the well, perhaps seeking Abuelo's company or some fresh air. His sullen look, a new norm for him, made him increasingly indistinguishable from the absent-faced horde of the sórdidos. It saddened Abuelo to see the man deteriorate.

"Buenas tardes," Abuelo said softly, before resuming his whistling as they passed each other on the path.

José Antonio froze. In a sudden spasm that sent Abuelo lurching backward, he howled, covering his ears. Abuelo reached out to the haunted man, but José Antonio refused him. "*Nunca más. Nunca más.* Never again."

His presence was doing more harm than help. There was no way to know what had triggered the fit, and no way to reach a sórdido caught in the hell of memory. With a final pat of José Antonio's convulsing shoulder, Abuelo continued toward the Casa.

He marched into the kitchen, expecting to see Doña Margarita's face light up at the sight of the clear water in his pail. Instead, she met him with a pained look.

"Doña!" He hoisted the pail onto the cracked countertop. "Look. El agua. It's clear!"

"Gracias." She wiped down the countertop where the water had splashed. "The United Nations Parliament brings many wonders to our world."

Abuelo rested his elbows on the counter. "What's on your mind, Margarita?"

Doña Margarita continued wiping the countertop, though it was clear there was nothing left to wipe. "Aleja came by earlier, while you were out walking. She wants you to meet with her as soon as possible."

Abuelo straightened with interest. "I thought she wasn't coming back until next week."

Doña Margarita wrung the liquid from the rag. "She said it was urgent."

"At the usual place, then?"

Doña continued wiping, refusing to look him in the eye. "No, she said you would know where. A place of ghosts, whatever that means."

Abuelo squared his shoulders. The bunker beneath the temple of Chaak. That must be where Aleja meant.

"She says she knows who you are."

Abuelo gently set his palms atop her hands. Doña Margarita turned away from him, her hands flying to her face. A tortured noise erupted from her throat and she looked at him with pleading eyes. "Maybe it doesn't matter who you were."

"What is it?" Abuelo probed, watching in horror as the unbreakable woman cracked.

"This isn't my house, Abuelo." She reached out to touch Abuelo's arm. "I heard about this place where lost souls gathered after the war. I came here looking for them. My Roberto, mi esposo, and our children."

She tossed the washcloth in the sink, and turned to Abuelo, eyes glistening. "When I met you, I thought that maybe, beneath those scars, you might be him." Her fingernails gently grazed the side of his face. "And when the news came from the government that they found the bodies of my family in a mass grave, I refused to believe it."

Waves of sorrow erupted from her as she collapsed against him. He held her, the woman who had cared for him tirelessly since he'd arrived. "I stayed here with you. To take care of you, and José Antonio, and the others. The ones without anyone to care for them."

Onlookers gathered in the sala — if they remembered anything it was this particular sorrow.

"I chose to pretend. But with you likely returning to your family, I must face the truth. I am alone," Margarita said, her face still pressed against his chest.

"Doña, I'm sorry he did this to you … to all of us," Abuelo murmured, enveloping her as if to shield her from the sórdidos gathering around them. "In the end we had you to save our souls, to show us that there is some light left in this wretched world."

She withdrew from his embrace, perhaps embarrassed by the audience. "Vaya con Dios," she whispered.

Go with God, he repeated to himself. *To which god do you refer?*

Abuelo kissed her cheek. "No matter what she tells me, I'll come back to you."

Doña shook her head, her lips creased with desperation.

"I have lived a lifetime of forgetting," Abuelo said as he turned for the door. "I think I'll spend what's left of it remembering."

The night before, Abuelo had written the remembered melody down on a sheet of scrap paper and had studied the pattern late into the evening, grateful to the family he didn't remember for the music lessons they had gifted him. Now, on his way to meet Aleja, he hummed the tune.

Harmonic echo vowels. Vigesimal meter.

The hill that housed the temple was steeper than he anticipated. Seeking respite from an arduous climb, he found shade beneath a ceremonial platform. As he sipped his water flask, he studied the faded, yet colorful glyphs painted along the cracked columns that supported the platform.

Chaak, the fanged deity. He who brings rain.

A fetid odor drew his gaze to the cool soil beneath his feet.

Impossible.

Green ferns spooled up from the earth, somehow spared the agony of the hydrophage.

They draw water from the cenote.

Then, above, he noticed the pale tubules and creeping shoots of a bromeliad, terminating in a strange crab-like flower. It made him think

59

of the sea — those tides of memory shifting within him.

Abuelo approached the steel-plated doors of the bunker, comforted by the screeching of the rusty hinges as he pushed his way through. The mechanism of the murky well at the Casa had called out in much the same way.

The vault within was not entirely dark. Aging fluorescent panels created pools of silvery light that revealed wafting pink dust. Abuelo passed chrome racks of servers arrayed in alternating rows like books stacked on library shelves. He moved past display cases where yellowing pamphlets and fragments of government documents had been meticulously arrayed. This was the work of an adept archivist.

Ahead, the vault tunneled into an ancient cave carved into the limestone by groundwater. As the steel tiles beneath his feet transitioned to wet stone, he passed into a hall lined with collages of framed photographs, passports, and moldy government-issued identification cards set on wooden easels. Victims of the purge. Their faces flickered in ghostly fluorescence — defiant, determined to be remembered in spite of the attempt to crumble their memory into dust.

"The dead won't go quietly," Aleja said, emerging as a sinuous shape at the dark edge of the chamber.

"An impressive archive," Abuelo said. "I assume this is your handiwork?" He approached one of the easels, where black mold had so stained a man's face that he scarcely looked human. Could the mold remember who it had consumed?

Though Aleja's expression was shadowed by the oversized hood of her sleeveless tunic, something on her face glinted. Without so much as a glance at him, Aleja opened a wooden chest to reveal a phonograph — an antique machine that must have been out of commission well before the war. She set the needle gently in place.

"What you seek is hidden." Abuelo grinned. "Encoded in music … it was entrusted to me." As if anticipating his whistle, an orchestral score filled the chamber, a soaring crescendo repeating the pattern he had been whistling for days.

Echo vowels.

"The Maya writing system is logosyllabic," Abuelo explained, remembering what he had scrawled the night before. Something in him wanted to please Aleja, to show her what he'd uncovered about himself. "For years, archaeologists misunderstood the nature of the glyphs. They represent ideas but they also indicate syllables. You see, they deciphered a peculiar glyph that functions like a repeat sign in music. Like poetry, the frequency and spacing of these repeats reflect a deliberate pattern. This melody corresponds to a passage in one of the surviving codices. But there is a hidden calculus behind the repetition."

Dresden codex. Page 7. A canid, jaws bared.

"Coordinates," Aleja surmised, approaching slowly, the mantle of shadow receding in her wake. Her arms, which in the six months of their time together she had carefully concealed with long sleeves, were webbed with melted skin. Without her wig, prosthetics, and thick makeup, the bloated knots of her nose and lips glistened in the faint lighting. Even without her hood fully drawn back, he could see that her bare scalp was as striated as his was. Her eyes devoured light as voraciously as before. "A new version of the National Anthem composed for the Reyes regime at the direction of the Caudillo himself."

Nunca más.

Abuelo picked at his hairless scalp. "The rebels must have played it at their rallies … to fuel their rage."

Nodding, Aleja turned to face the darkest part of the chamber, a portal to what he suspected was a vast network of caverns. "Do you remember why they painted themselves red?"

Somewhere in the darkness, Abuelo perceived a fluttering of winged things, bats roosting in the dark fissures of the vault.

Aleja ignored his silence, pacing the perimeter with her hands tucked behind her back. "UN observers say we were inspired by Novemberist revolutionaries in Siberia. That we went red as part of a global left-wing resurgence." She approached a lectern where the faces of the condemned looked back at her. "But to anyone who remembers with their bones, they know red to be a symbol of our people in the ages before the Caudillo, the Congress, and the Conquistadores."

Looking at Aleja now made his own skin flare with remembered heat, so he diverted his gaze from the wounds that scored her body. "Red, like the temple of the Red Wolf, what the Maya called le kiäqa utiw," he said, closing his eyes to visualize the stelae and murals of an ancient temple. Abuelo dug into his pocket and handed her the paper on which he had scrawled the coordinates, a simple calculation based on the distances between notes in the score. "The weapon cache is buried there … I remember."

"Excellent," Aleja said, already typing the coordinates into a computer console beside her. "My people will verify your intel momentarily. Until then, it's time for your final dose of medication." She walked over to the wooden chest again, a smile edging her lips as she retrieved a bottle of bourbon and two cigars. As she poured the amber liquor into the glasses, the smoky sweet aroma stirred up curious feelings. When Abuelo closed his eyes, images flowed unbidden.

Drinks in the parlor, sea breeze tickling his skin — flowing through white curtains, rustling the long black hair of a woman and her daughter. Mirror images of each other. They peer at him with black eyes.

Abuelo gasped, forcing his eyes open.

"My hope is that this place will conjure up lost memories." She caressed the pane of glass that encased the photographs and documents, as if to touch the faces of the dead. She lifted a photograph from the easel and set it before him. A family smiled back at him. The father's chiseled tawny-red face a lighter hue than the deep ochre of the mother and daughter. There was something striking about the girl's eyes. Something familiar.

"I've seen them before."

Aleja struck a match, puffing a cigar into a tobacco incense. White fumes wreathed her dark features. She handed him one, watching as, with slow inhalations, he instinctively drew the tobacco into glowing embers.

"That girl," he said, exhaling a plume of wispy smoke. "It's you."

Aleja studied him in silence, the serpentine trail of her smoke entwining with his. He imagined her as a child, running through sunlit halls. He imagined her mother, sipping cocktails in a marble veranda by the sea. But he could not see the mestizo man in the photograph. He could not remember him as he could the mother and the daughter.

"Hector Beltrán Rosa," Abuelo said at last, pacing the same perimeter Aleja had. Whereas she had been assured and upright, Abuelo was increasingly agitated. "José Antonio once said there was no body to bury, only ashes. That he and his family were killed on the eve of the rebel victory." Abuelo stopped, suddenly unsure if he was thinking aloud. "I can't remember him because *he* is me."

Abuelo tossed his cigar into the ash tray. "Mija!" He gripped her shoulders. They'd been precisely in this position when she was a child, he was sure of it. In this way he'd imparted important lessons or chastised her if she deserved it. In this way, he'd loved her. "I remember you — yes — I know you."

"I *am* his daughter." She pulled away from his desperate embrace, shifting her attention to a display case. "Before the war, my father worked with the Caudillo at the university." Aleja knelt down to fish for something inside the case. "They were friends once, if you can believe that. United by their shared fascination with the distant past. Frequent guests at each other's homes, though the Caudillo never had time or interest in having a family of his own. And it is through that friendship that Beltrán Rosa played both sides, building this place so that no one would ever forget the horrors of the war his friend turned Caudillo had wrought."

The room reeled with Abuelo's sudden nausea. The bourbon. He couldn't remember the last time he had alcohol. Steadying himself with one hand on the display case, he looked up to find that the faces in the photographs were glaring at him. He refused to meet their unblinking eyes.

Never again.

"There are those who wonder if Beltrán sold our people out to foreigners to achieve his victory. Those UN imperialists who want nothing short of our sovereignty in exchange for cleaning up the hydrophage." Aleja opened a glass case, reached for another crumpled photograph. "There are some who wonder if our victory is actually defeat. Who knows what those UN drones are spraying on our land? You must have seen the ferns growing under the temple — the only place where their fertilizer doesn't reach."

Abuelo steadied himself against the lectern. "Surely the UN have come to help. Why else would they ... I don't understand, mija. Why do you recoil from me?" He reached for her hand but she retreated again. Dizzy, he stumbled until he found a moldy armchair at the edge of the chamber. He sat, breathing hard into the dark maw of the cavern beyond.

Aleja's voice deepened. "Do you feel it? The pull of the past?"

"Fire." Abuelo struggled to speak — his throat was suddenly so dry. "The Fire."

"Yes, I survived it," said Aleja, the hook of flesh that was her nose seeming to contort with her sneer.

Men in fatigues, machetes streaming with blood. A woman and her child, bloodied and beaten, thrown into the fire. Smoldering flesh. The foul scent of burning hair.

"Your mother, they're killing her," he muttered.

All at once, the computer screens around the room flickered with notifications. Aleja rushed to the closest terminal and spoke a language he did not understand into its microphone. Abuelo hunched forward in his chair, fighting the urge to vomit. He looked up to find Aleja standing in front of him, her face a blur in his compromised vision.

"Your intel checks out, Abuelo. We officially beat the Androvirus!" With a heartier laugh than he had ever heard from her, she raised her glass. "A toast, then?" She refilled his drink and passed it to him. "To the immortal past!"

Abuelo clinked glasses with Aleja. "It's finally over … the terrorists lost?"

Letting Abuelo's words dissipate without response, Aleja mounted a camera onto a tripod, framed him in the shot and set it to record. Perhaps she wanted to document their victory, a father and daughter reunited at last. A flashing light announced the machine's broadcasting status.

"Did you know that some people deliberately infect themselves with Androvirus?" Aleja said between puffs of her cigar. "People who are too cowardly to take their own lives. People whose deeds in life are too much for them to bear."

She dropped a photograph into his lap. In the familiar, gaunt face of the man in the frame he saw the death squads, his macheteros. He felt the pen in his hand, felt the ink flowing as he signed executive orders, as he created the labor camps, as he staged addresses to congress, and initiated the Desagüe, his campaign of total desiccation. His genocide.

"Gonzalo Ocasio Reyes," he said to himself at last.

"*That* name is something of a curse these days." Aleja said through bared teeth. "But I delivered your past as promised. Unfortunately, there is no family for you to be reunited with. The Caudillo never took a wife, never had children and any persons with the surnames Reyes or Ocasio were hunted down by your macheteros and killed in cold blood. You made it clear there would be no heirs to compete for your throne."

"I was supposed to forget. They said I would forget!" Gonzalo bellowed with clenched fists. With rending clarity, he remembered it all. Signing the death warrants of his relatives. Turning on the peasants that elected him. He remembered the flames he wielded against the traitors and those savage indios that abetted them. He remembered the desiccant he used to kill his world.

We could have been the envy of the globe. If only they had let go of the past. If only they had looked to the future. It's their fault. They forced my hand. They are like children. They had to be punished.

"It was near the end of your reign that you figured out that you had a traitor in your midst. So you ordered your men to round up my family and burn us alive. You were there, watching with satisfaction, as I recall." Aleja swayed back and forth, as if staging a re-enactment. "Your troops left me there to burn. They didn't bother to finish me off. I don't think they had the stomach for it."

Gonzalo coughed, blood coating the back of his throat.

Aleja took another swig of bourbon. "The walls were closing in on you. They were coming and, the pendejo that you were, you decided to hide yourself in one of your own labor camps. Disfigured by your own hand to appear unrecognizable, until the virus spared you the memory of living with what you've done."

"Water," he whimpered, writhing in his chair. His body was burning from the inside out. It had seemed like perfect logic then. The only way to kill the past was to turn it to dust. So that's what he did. To free his people from the primitivism they refused to let go.

Aleja crossed her scarred arms. "You wanted to evaporate into the clouds, ignorant and unknowing, freed from the burden of your deeds. But you underestimated how much my father knew you — the kind of man you were. Feckless. He knew this would be how you would try to escape your end."

"How did you find me?"

Aleja's dark eyes flared with contempt. "I followed the trail my father left behind. This archive. These documents."

Gonzalo gritted his teeth against the contractions in his throat, his lungs. What right did she have to judge him? "Are you going to kill me?" he spat.

"I already have."

Gonzalo slid from the chair onto the floor, his sight blurred, still fixed on Aleja. A moment ago, he had fancied himself her father. It hadn't been an unpleasant fiction. But now that other imprisoned within him was free and along with him the catalogue of his hatred. People like Aleja were the reason they could never progress. Fucking Indians. He'd wasted so much time studying their kind, trying to find anything redeemable in their barbaric past. He'd found nothing. Nothing.

She held up his glass, which he could now see was stained red. "I gave you just enough of the blight so you could feel the moisture vanish from your body. Just enough for you to burn without fire."

Gonzalo thrashed on the cold ground. They'd called him Abuelo. But how could he reconcile his new experiences with his old life — his time among the sórdidos, and his time as the one who created them. José Antonio. Margarita. Casa Sórdida. Their suffering was his legacy. And yet they were the only family he had ever known.

Abuelo. Such a ridiculous name. You might have died never knowing what you really are, in that shithole with those filthy peasants. Eating their food. Sleeping with —

His breath clawed up from his throat like a starved animal. "I only wanted to free our people from those cabrónes who would stop at nothing short of owning the world." His dry tongue clicked with every syllable. "It was the Spaniards who invented the Desagüe in Tenochtitlan, half a millennium ago. To dry out the stinking swamp of savagery. Like them, we were choking on the stench of the indio. The hydrophage was the cure." Gonzalo buried his face in his hands. "Hector was weak. He fell in love with one of them. Had a child with one of them. I should have finished you off when I had the chance."

Aleja regarded him in silence, eyes watering with fury. "Even as you take your last breaths, all you have is your hate and fear of us." The fluorescent lights flickered as she unzipped her hoodie and threw back the cowl that covered her bald head.

"But you are right to fear us, Caudillo. We are survivors. We survived the Spanish, we survived Rios Mont and his predecessors, and we survived you." Aleja thumbed a nearby console. One by one, a series of floodlights drenched the room with amber light, the percussive echo of their ignition scattering a flock of bats. Above the flapping of their wings, their trilling cries, Aleja spoke, half to him, and half to the audience to which her camera was broadcasting.

"Today the fire of the Maya is rekindled." She gestured to the chamber's newly illuminated walls, which were etched with the bright turquoise whorls of feathered quetzals, the black and ochre of glyphic scripts, too crisp and vibrant to not be artificially augmented. He realized the lights doubled as projectors, restoring the color in glyphs muddied by centuries of tropical decay.

Aleja faced the camera, her arms sweeping as she spoke. "Here in the dirt and squalor, this *sordidez* that you and the conquistadores left us to rot in, a new civilization takes root. The Yucatán will once again bloom Maya red."

Dresden codex. Page 7. A canid, jaws bared.

Aleja turned to Gonzalo. "We come out of the shadows, we swarm and flock under the banner of kiäqa utiw, the red wolf. And with your weapons, we will remake the world in our own image."

She waded into a cone of golden light. With his bleary vision, her raised arms looked like wings, as if she were a vengeful angel sent to usher him into the afterlife. Below her collar bone, in the scarred mat of flesh where her breasts had been cut out by machetes, a beast's fangs gleamed in carmine ink. It hungered for his flesh.

"What —" he slurred, his breath thick with blood as his flameless immolation neared completion. "What are you?"

"Your legacy," Aleja declared. Behind her, a pair of priests emerged, their coppery bodies ornamented with turquoise, hair braided into colorful headdresses and conical shapes. In unison, they rapped the cave floor with bone staffs as she drew closer. "The Queen that was slumbering."

Then came her soldiers, wolf-men, their bodies sheened with crimson paint, obsidian blades gleaming in the glow of ancient glyphs. "La Caudilla."

Heat. Such cruel heat. His sweat was boiling.

"Le kiäqa utiw."

As his skin melted, he could hear something howl in the darkness.

"La Loba Roja."

• • •

ch'aqa palo | across the sea

"The cause for which the Christians have slain and destroyed so many
… has been simply to get, as their ultimate end, the Indians' gold of
them … owing to the insatiable greed and ambition that they have
had, which has been greater than any the world has ever seen before."

Bartolomé de las Casas, *An Account of the Destruction of the Indies*,
1552 CE

Hidden in the gnarled grooves and rosy spindles of lead-
woods, a chorus slumbered. As dusk fell on Borikén,
liming the talon-like roots of the mangroves with copper
mist, the frogs sang. Call and response. An amphibian bomba, the slick
amber of their bodies rising and falling with each exultation.

At least we still have the coquis, Anacaona thought, as the target
came into view. The tranquil music of the tree frogs she and Yuíza used
to hunt as children never failed to soothe her, especially on nights like
this, when she was anxious.

If our intel is right, this will be a feast.

Anacaona approached the ivory capsule half-submerged in brackish waters. Yuíza followed close behind, with Dagüao taking up the rear. He carried a heavy pack filled with the equipment they would need to pilfer the United Nations Parliament. Yuíza's studied the capsule, then shifted her gaze to Anacaona.

Is my anxiety that obvious?

Anacaona smiled bitterly at her sister. No, she wasn't being obvious. It was Yuíza. She had a gift. Anacaona wondered if she had inherited their grandmother Serafína's prescience, induced in dreams after long nights of incense-fueled prayer to her Orishas and a bowl of water she called Madre Agua. Or had it been passed down from their grandfather Abey, a descendant of Taíno shamans?

Dagüao splashed through the water ahead of them. -Don't touch,- Dagüao signed before scanning the target with a modified smartphone camera. Yuíza caught up with him and rested her chin on his shoulder, studying the infrared scan.

-Looks good,- she announced.

Anacaona was always envious of Yuíza's multilingual finesse. The smoothness of her English. The precision and fluidity of her signs when she communicated with Doña Marta or Dagüao, who became Anacaona's adopted little brother the moment that Yuíza brought him home from school to meet their family. That was ages ago. Before Teddy. Before the Cacicazgo. Before their blood brother abandoned them without a parting glance.

-What has it?- Anacaona queried clumsily. Dagüao smirked, but she could tell he appreciated the effort. Signing while out on a mission was no longer about being inclusive to their fellow guajires-in-arms who could not hear. They had learned from the tragic outcome of a previous supply raid that the enemy had planted listening devices around critical supply caches.

As long as I don't end up like the Anacaona. Slaughtered by colonizers at a peace banquet.

71

Dagüao leapt up excitedly. -Molecular storage kit,- his interlaced fingers parting to mimic the proteins he was referring to in ASL.

Anacaona did not need to sign to convey her complete and utter lack of understanding of Dagüao's geek-speak. Her face was expressive enough.

Yuíza translated, whispering in their revived Island Arawak. "I think he wants to turn our ceibas into living computers."

-Very cool, no?- Dagüao signed with a toothy smile.

Anacaona tried to her mask her disappointment. More tech was great, but they needed to keep the lights on. They needed food.

-Power cells!- Yuíza signed, as the plastichrome fibers encasing the cache unspooled, revealing the contents within.

Anacaona smirked. -God is good.-

They secured the spoils in their jaba, kapok sacks they slung over their shoulders. As darkness deepened, they marveled at the sapphire sheen coating tree trunks, and glowing in starry whorls at their feet. A feat of scientific sorcery engineered by their resident nerds, Dagüao and Yuíza, to light their way at night. The dinoflagellates had been genetically altered to thrive on dewy surfaces as well as the salty inlets in which they'd lived for generations.

Dagüao's eyes brightened. -Beautiful.-

The alarm tripped as Anacaona reached for the last of the power cells. "Time to move!" she shouted to Yuíza over the blare of the klaxon.

Dagüao was still fiddling with glittering vials of synthetic DNA. -Almost done,- he signed, noticing the flashing alarm.

Yuíza opened her tablet, scanning for incoming signals. Anacaona looked on with her, confirming her worst fears.

The feast is on and we're what's for dinner.

"Carajo!" Yuíza cursed, staring at steadily approaching heat signatures. "Missionaries incoming."

"As good a time as any to test countermeasures." Anacaona turned to Dagüao. -Start the party,- she signed to him.

Dagüao puffed his chest in an exaggerated display of machismo. -Let them come,- he signed.

Yuíza helped him unravel the countermeasures from the tarp. She laughed out loud. "Ana, he brought masks. Dagüao must think the missionaries are coming for Carnival."

"They've come for blood." Anacaona brandished her macana. The club was fashioned from the hardened roots of a ceiba, but thanks to Yuíza's tinkering, it doubled as a stun baton. A replacement for the modded sledgehammer she'd broken while smashing cryptomansions.

-How will these masks save us?- Yuíza signed, fearful as she readied her blowgun and seeker darts.

Anacaona peered into the tarp. -Dagüao honors the ancestors,- Her gaze sifted past the brilliant colors, horns, razor-edged teeth, polka-dotted spines, and settled on the simplest design wrought from buffed ochre and hardwood — the trigonic head of a cemí, a three-faced slumbering deity of the Taíno, its highest tip jutting up like a shark tooth.

-Your father,- Yuíza signed to him, remembering the man's workshop in Ponce, a mess of paints, paper-maché, and frightful visages crafted to ward off hungry demons. She elected for the mask in the obiwayza style, wrought from a coconut shell, strewn with the bright yellow, green, and reds of the flag of Loíza, the town of her namesake.

-This will work,- Dagüao signed as a terrifying aspect covered his face. With his curved horns, ghoulish eyes, and jagged teeth, Dagüao had transformed into a Vejigante, a guardian sent from the spirit world to deliver them from the mechanical monstrosities that hunted them. Dagüao clutched his spiked pelota, a modified version of the rubber ball he built to entertain the children in their cancha.

Let them come.

73

Anacaona imagined they must have looked like a trio of fiends as they lined up in the shimmering dusk, weapons poised to strike. She could already hear the missionaries whirring through the mangroves.

It's our turn to feast.

She wanted to close her eyes as the pellucid swarms got within a hair's distance of them, but she held her ground. The hideous armada converged on their position, their plastichrome tentacles probing the air like cybernetic perversions of jellyfish. Silvery proboscises lanced out of their mouths, dripping as they poised to strike but did not. Instead, they floated in place, appraising the thieves, evidently trans-fixed by their masks. One by one, they twitched and flitted out of control, as if merely beholding the Vejigantes had paralyzed them.

"Now!" Anacaona bellowed, slamming her macana into the near-est missionary, white sparks blooming. Dagüao hurled his barbed pelota, laughing maniacally as the smart weapon pummeled their tentacled foes into oblivion, bouncing from one to another like a pin-ball. Yuíza did not gloat as she shot down the last of the cnidarian drones, lowering her blowgun warily.

What are you sensing from the beyond, hermanita?

With the masks' augmented reality visors, they could communi-cate via text on their short-range wireless network. =That was amazing, Dag, how did you do it?=

Dagüao surveyed the smoking remains of wrecked drones like a demon searching for souls to take with him to hell. =I hacked the image recognition algorithms. Downloaded the code from one of the missionaries we captured in Vegabaja. I used it to encrypt a subroutine that would override primary functions, triggered by a unique image of my design. Like those QR codes they used back in the 2010s. Clever isn't it?=

=¡Qué gufiao!= Yuíza typed into her wristpad.

"What's wrong Yuíza? Scanners are clear." As she spoke, Anacaona felt the ground shift beneath her feet. This wasn't like the earthquakes she had experienced at their aunt's house in Guánica. This was something else. Something big.

=Proximity alert.= Yuíza looked up.

Anacaona waded through the salt marsh, searching for signs of their elusive enemy. =Thermal signatures. They're =

Yuíza studied her tablet, tracking moving blobs of thermal energy, taking up too much of the map. =Gigantic.=

These aren't missionaries. They're something else. Something worse.

Dagüao clutched his pelota. =If they are what I think they are. Masks won't work=

The waters around them rippled with each new vibration.

=Ana, what do we do now? = Yuíza tugged at her sister's elbow.

=Do we surrender?= Dagüao added.

Instinctively the trio had moved into a defensive formation and now Dagüao's back pressed against Anacaona's. He was trembling. Ahead, Anacaona glimpsed something white through the bioluminescent canopies.

I won't go the way of Cacica Anacaona. I won't be killed while trying to make peace with monsters. I'll die fighting. I'll die a rebel.

"We fight!" Anacaona removed her mask. As their gargantuan shadows enveloped her, she stood her ground, macana raised, eyes unflinching. There was no running this time. She could not save Yuíza or Dagüao or the yucayeke or what was left of the cacicazgo. But she could fight. She could remain until the very end. She could do what Vero never did.

····

diluvio | deluge

"The miserable ones were all pierced through; they were alive though
they had no hearts. Then they were buried in the sands — there would
be a sudden rush of water ... then the sky would fall, it would fall
down upon the earth, when the four Bacabs, were set up, who brought
about the destruction of the world."

Chilam Balam of Chumayel, circa 1700 CE

Afternoon crept into the room, bathing the cobwebs in the
window with soft light. With a feather duster, Margarita
flicked a cascade of dust motes from the concrete sill where
thick clumps of sand had caked. No matter how much effort she put
into the task, the airborne silts of the Yucatán desert would always find
their way back. But she maintained this futile routine; the image of
order it produced, however fleeting, filled with her a sense of control
and possibility. She took comfort knowing that her efforts could bring
a sliver of serenity to otherwise difficult days. War elevated the basest
of comforts.

The air quivered around her and Margarita froze. These vibrations were now so rare that she found them frightening. She peered through spidering cracks in the window to the parched earth beyond, where shadow dappled the ground. Her arthritic joints ached in a once-familiar anticipation. When the noise sounded again, Margarita dropped her duster and bolted outside to bear witness to the spectacle that had become a distant memory.

Another klaxon cleaved the sky. Her nostrils flared, tickled by the aroma of ozone. The sórdidos came clambering out of their tin-roofed shacks and concrete caves to behold the wonder gathering above.

In the sky, gray shapes plumed into lenticular formations, like a fleet of warships converging on an ethereal foe. They soon unleashed their coruscating volleys, azure and white lances crisscrossing the heavens. The land was awakening, veins of blue electricity a defibrillator for the necrotic flesh of the Caudillo's desert. Then, audible above the clamor of thunder, she heard a collective gasp as lightning gave way to moisture. The wet beads were so hot that at first they evaporated before they hit the earth.

The onlookers held their gazes to the surging skies. Margarita broke into wild laughter. The sound of it startled her as it pitched higher, as she found her body twirling, arms lifting to welcome the waters.

As the heavy rain pummeled her, as the beads dissolved into vapor that kissed the back of her neck, she wondered if she was dreaming. The sudden humidity transported her to her childhood, to nights when she was ill and her Tzeltal mother carried her into a lemongrass steam bath to warm her blood.

"The United Nations Parliament brings many wonders to our land!" Margarita yelled at the swirling clouds, as if conversing with God.

One of the elder sórdidos fell to his knees in genuflection. Many followed, offering their gratitude to the Virgén, the Holy Father, or

Chaak, the rain deity with many names. Their staggered prayers mirrored the cadence of the falling rain as it hammered the tin roofs of the compound. Then she heard another sound that had receded from memory. Over the rataplan of rain it was there, rising steadily. She scanned the skies for the source of this miracle, wiping her eyes to get a better look. Amidst the downpour that fell like molten glass, the sórdidos had joined hands. Their lips were moving.

How could I have forgotten?

The sórdidos sang an old folk song Margarita remembered in her bones. From those days in Chiapas, when it was still México, when she was a little girl who chased hens, who whispered to sheaves of blonde maize because she still believed they were where people came from. Before her, the sórdidos transformed from a lifeless horde to an enchanted choir. In that moment, she forgot that the world had ever been wrong.

She strolled past the last of the thatched huts and makeshift shelters, and approached Jose Antonio's flower beds, savoring the petrichor fragrance rising from the soil. Not long ago, they'd stood here together, sweating from the exertion of the build, doubting that flowers would ever grow again. Now she inclined her head to the flickering sky, admiring its turbulent industry.

Help this land remember what it used to be.

The earth was thirsty enough to bleed. Water sluiced through wounds in the xeric landscape, scoring the vermillion clays and bleached silts as it went. Spirals of reddish milk oozed up from the dirt, the last defiant remnants of the hydrophage striving but failing to repel the overwhelming deluge. With the baptism bubbling around her, Margarita noticed that Abuelo's pail was nearly full. She hadn't dared to move it since she'd buried him.

"Abuelo, you won't have to walk far today to bring us water," she said softly. "I wish you were here to experience this beauty with us, my old friend. Did you send it our way, from the other side?"

She kept her eyes shut, trying her best not to remember how he looked when she discovered him in the vault. After her screams had subsided, Ismael and Ximena had watched in horror as she yelled at his corpse. "I told you not to go!" The young ones had helped her carry his shriveled body. He was as light as the frayed documents and photographs they found piled around him. A paper cadaver.

He had taken his own life by ingesting a concentrated amount of the hydrophage. There was enough of it in the landscape if you knew where to look. Like so many of the sórdidos she had come to know and care for over the years, he had learned the terrible truth that he was alone, that there was no family for him but the ones at the Casa. The truth — that he was another forgettable, unimportant person — had shattered him. The woman from the government had only promised him his past, not happiness or significance.

"I am sorry we never made you feel like part of *this* family," she whispered.

She was ashamed to admit she had ever felt envious of Abuelo. Androvirus spared him the trauma of the war that so many still carried. When at last he felt what everyone else felt, it crushed him in an instant. He didn't last a single day in this hell that she and the others had endured for so long. Did that make her stronger? She doubted that. There were days when her bones felt heavier, as if gravity had doubled. Those were the days she remembered her own family. Beside Abuelo's cross in the Casa's humble cemetery, they rested. The bodies of her husband and children had been identified in a mass grave outside Quetzal, one of the Caudillo's most notorious internment camps. She had transferred them here.

"It was raining then, too, the last time God let me see your faces," Margarita said to their crosses.

The rain was different then. There had been a turbulent, sinister quality to the downpour that fell after the first of the hydrophage detonations. When the deluge subsided, moisture dissipated so rapidly from the hot soil that lightning spawned, kindling wildfires that blackened the lush hills and valleys of their country. It was an evening not unlike this one when the tainted rains fell, and the Caudillo's hunters came for them announcing that their family farm now belonged to the Reyes regime. When her Roberto refused to comply, they beat him until his face was purple. Margarita had intervened, convincing the soldiers not to take his life. Her children had clutched her blood-spattered huipil all the way to the work camps.

The train that carried them rattled through the night, but the family remained together. Elena and Mariel kept vigil between choked sobs, while her youngest, Bastian, fell in and out of sleep. When they arrived at their destination, the Caudillo's men announced that Margarita would be stationed at a women's munitions camp in Flores, while the rest of her family would remain at Quetzal. The rain was still falling as she clutched them for the last time. Her daughters wailed while her son stood stiff as a stone.

"I'll find you," her Roberto had said as he kissed her forehead. "I will not rest until I do."

He never got the chance to look. Instead, after the Lobos liberated her from Flores, it was she who set out in search of them. For years, she scoured the country, consulting the official registries and the first censuses conducted by the People's Government. Her travels delivered her to a forgotten bit of real estate where the hydrophage had struck hardest. The place where only the most broken and destitute gathered. There she established El Centro de Refugiados.

"Doña Margarita!" Ximena called over the din of the rain. Margarita shook her head, clearing away the lingering memories.

"Isn't it beautiful?" Margarita said, looking up again at the rumbling sky. Young people always managed to rekindle her optimism.

Ximena's boots squelched in the thickening mud. Ismael followed her, strands of his wet hair sticking to his face.

"Doña Margarita, look! Inundación!" Ximena cried, pointing to a what looked like a brown mountain steadily bearing down on them from the mouth of the valley.

A deluge.

"¡Diós mío!" Margarita started for the Casa and the old public address system, hoping the microphone still worked. "I'll make the announcement. In the meantime, bring everyone into the sala, where the foundations are higher."

The rain continued for two weeks. Mud flowed from the hills, exposing more of the buried Maya ruins. A moat of umber waters encircled the Casa Sórdida, as if it were chosen to withstand the wrath of a cleansing God. Ximena drew on her engineering talents to construct a raft out of recovered debris, with the help of Ismael and a few others with mechanical know-how. When she first arrived at the Casa, Ximena, then a young orphan, had apprenticed herself to Don Luis, the Casa's handyman. When Margarita had asked her why a young woman would take an interest in such a thing, Ximena had said, "Fixing things reminds me that the world can be changed."

Ismael and Ximena used their raft to patrol the waters, looking for valuable jetsam carried from upstream. Since the flood, the UN delegation had not delivered their weekly shipment of supplies. Margarita had prepared for their eventual abandonment, creating a cache of foodstuffs, medicines, and other supplies. No one had noticed the sacrifices they'd been making all along, the cans or bags of flour that she had been stockpiling, depriving them of extra helpings with these desperate days in mind. As the Casa's stores dwindled, she thanked her past self for her prudence.

From the roof that had become their lookout tower, she peered across the floodplain. On the radio, they had overheard static-laced murmurings of violence springing up all over the countryside. The People's Government claimed a terrorist was at large, using the chaos of the storm as cover for vast seizures of land. History was repeating itself. Another wave of war to follow the mud. She knew that war would come again, that the People's Government would fail as they were failing her now, but she hadn't expected it so soon.

Avian shapes bristled on the horizon. Atop their raft, Ximena and Ismael waved as aircraft soared over the mud-streaked hills in a tight formation. They touched down on a promontory of rock that loomed over the floodwaters. Soon the silty lake was teeming with an armada of inflated rafts.

Margarita and the others descended from the roof to greet the United Nations peacekeepers on their makeshift dock. Their white regalia seemed too bright for the grayness of this world. They formed close ranks as they approached, parting to allow a tall man in a military uniform to pass to the front of their rank. The red and gold brassard on his arm signaled that he was an agent of the People's Government rather than a UN operative. Even in the wan light of overcast skies, Margarita could see that his skin was pale, like sun-bleached oak, and his eyes were a rare shade of viridian that exuded kindness. He stopped short of entering the Casa, his cheeks dimpling as he smiled at Margarita.

"Margarita Urbina Soto?"

She nodded, noting how the young man stooped when he spoke to her, as if to meet her halfway.

"I hear you call the shots around here?"

"Someone has to," Margarita said, bowing her head slightly, a gesture that felt especially ridiculous given his stature.

"We've been looking for you." He extended his hand. "You can call me Juaco."

She shook his offered hand. "You're with the People's Government."

"Yes," Juaco said with a nod. "My apologies we could not come sooner. But we're here to help."

Animated by a signal from Juaco, the peacekeepers moved into the compound, wheeling in crates of supplies from the rafts. Spherical drones bobbed behind them.

"We are grateful," Margarita said.

"I'm glad I found you." Juaco's eyes narrowed as he studied her. The tips of his long lashes glistened with beads of captured rain. Or were they tears?

Margarita had seen this sudden outpouring of emotion before. War could make kin of strangers. She had seen it among her sórdidos. The way they comforted each other in those quiet moments between emptiness and sorrow.

She clutched his forearm and Juaco straightened, his face flush with sudden embarrassment. "I'm sorry. It's just different than I expected, this place."

Margarita tugged at her wet huipil. "I'm surprised you know about it."

"They ran a story about you in the *Daily Harbinger*."

Vero Diaz. The reporter.

"I should be grateful. I was beginning to think your people had forgotten us." Margarita placed her hands on her hips. "Aleja said to expect supply runs more frequently."

Juaco raised an eyebrow. "Aleja?"

"One of yours. A young woman. Dark features. Deep voice," Margarita continued, noting a ripple of panic on Juaco's face. "Juaco?"

"This woman —" Juaco gripped her shoulders. "She was *here*?"

"Yes, she's been coming by for months." Margarita stepped aside for peacekeepers unloading supply crates. "She was helping someone here. A friend suffering from Andro. She promised treatment.

83

Something experimental."

Margarita's gaze drifted to the crosses jutting up from the muddy pool behind the Casa. "I don't know if the treatment worked. But whatever he discovered about his past, it drove him to — well —" She swallowed and masked her sorrow with a cough.

"I'm sorry." In his voice she heard something that sounded like anger. "You mourn him, then?"

It was a strange question for a stranger to ask and Margarita frowned. "I mourn every soul taken by this despicable war."

Juaco waved to one of the white-armored agents, who approached at his beckoning. "Señora Urbina, we need you to come with us."

"Why?" Margarita eyed the pearly capes of the peacekeepers. Was this a request or an order? She tilted her head toward the Casa. "My place is here, with my people."

Juaco held his arms out in supplication. "We need your help."

"Why? What can I do that you can't?" She gestured to the throngs of sórdidos now gathering outside. "These people count on me. I can't just leave."

"Then we bring them with us." Juaco pointed west, toward the printed spheres that were visible on a clear day. "This valley isn't safe anymore. There could be more landslides, everything could be washed away."

Margarita looked to the sórdidos, at the shabby sofas, and the kitchen she'd arranged just as she liked. She didn't want to leave, but she knew if she went the sórdidos would follow. "Where would you take us?"

"To the Green Zone. You'll be well cared for there."

Margarita shook her head. "I don't understand, joven. Why are you so frightened?"

"That *woman*," Juaco said, swallowing hard. "She is not who you think she is."

"She works with your government, doesn't she?"

"Margarita," Juaco turned to face her, his eyes wide. "There was a broadcast over UN channels. This Aleja, she's ... the Loba Roja."

She'd heard that name on the radio, but nothing about a broadcast. "Isn't that the terrorist you've been looking for?"

Juaco nodded. "You're in grave danger — had we known sooner, we would have already evacuated you."

But Margarita paid him no mind. She moved with a purpose, wading into clay-darkened waters, toward the back of the Casa. Lightning bloomed around her.

"Where are you going?" Juaco shouted as he pursued her.

She rounded the well and splashed into the dark waters of the graveyard. She sank to her knees before a cross jutting up from the murk.

"Abuelo," she whispered, above the crackling of thunder. "Forgive me. Forgive me for letting her deceive you. I will find the truth. If she is responsible for what happened to you, she will stand trial before God if it is the last thing I do on this Earth."

She felt Juaco's hands on her arms, his touch gentle, coaxing her up from the mud.

"You don't have to do it alone."

Margarita knew something of soft-hearted children, how soft hearts could grow into their strength. Despite his uniform, his display of rank, she could tell that Juaco's heart was soft. He'd fought because he'd had to. Maybe he was still fighting, still running from something. She didn't know what, but she did know that truths took their time. What mattered most now was that she needed him as much as he needed her.

A world raced beneath her feet. The pallid ghosts of desiccated forests shivered beneath sanguine flotsam. Fighting a sudden bout of vertigo, Margarita looked up to catch the animated expressions of the sórdidos, experiencing flight for the first time. No pilot sat at the helm of the craft.

"The United Nations Parliament brings many wonders to our country," she whispered to herself, like a prayer.

"The Green Zone is beyond those mountains," Juaco said, as their craft weaved between cloud and striated peaks.

With computational precision, the craft began its landing sequence, descending into a colossal sphere of glass. Even from this altitude she could make out clusters of modular structures and patches of green climbing up to kiss the sun. It reminded her of her chipilín in the kitchen: green shoots of possibility reaching up from the cola bottle she had fashioned into a planter.

Below, a circular pane of glass parted and they dipped into the sphere. When they set down, Margarita unfastened her seatbelt and followed Juaco down the landing ramp, trailed by her bewildered sórdidos. A tide of jubilation swept over their faces as they navigated the glass catwalk, flanked by vertically stacked hydroponic arrays that burst with color: the soft violet of budding baalche', pale gold plumeria, cerise orchids and green plantains. Below, water flowed through a canal flanked by terraced banks where royal palms, yellow oleanders and milky-blue jacarandas flourished in the open air. A cloud of warm mist rained down from above.

Juaco drew Margarita away from the hidden sprinklers, steering her toward a containerized habitat where maize swayed in an artificial breeze. "This is where we grow the food we send you." Juaco fought to be heard over the horn-like calls of a t'ho perched on a nearby oleander. "Most of the species are indigenous to the region."

Ismael tugged at Ximena's refajo, drawing her attention to a pair of yellow-bellied x'takay as they swooped down from the boughs of huejotes curling up from the canal's terraces. Margarita didn't think she'd ever seen them so happy.

"All this time you had this, while we …" She fell silent as she spotted the blurred wingspan of a hummingbird.

"Not everyone lives this way." Juaco stepped between her and the dazzling vista, gently directing her to continue along the path. "These printed facilities are too expensive to replicate on a nation-wide scale. The UN built these to address the famine while their drones work to neutralize the hydrophage in the land."

Margarita remembered the strange hum of the drones as they dumped their neutralizer over the parched hills by the Casa. They reminded her of the bees that used to buzz in her ears as she picked ciruelos in her orchard. Her children's favorite snack. "So these rains are the fruit of those efforts?"

"We believe so." Juaco gripped the railing as the path gently sloped toward a massive glass honeycomb structure. "Only time will tell."

Juaco paused at the base of the honeycomb, waiting for the excitement of the sórdidos to dissipate before speaking. "This will be your lodging during your time here." Walking backwards like a tour guide as the sórdidos followed, he smiled as his guests gawked at the stacked hexagonal cells of tinted glass above them. "Each domicile is fully stocked and has its own private terrace. Help yourselves to what grows there." Juaco gestured to the cross-hatching gables where green peeked through translucent panes.

The sórdidos cheered and clapped with excitement. Margarita looked at the abundance around her and frowned. She could never give them this. Feeling the warmth of her Casa slipping away, all she wanted was to go home.

"Margarita," Juaco held the door for the sórdidos who were shuffling into the complex, their sparse belongings carried in backpacks or duffels. "When you're settled in, find me by the baobab tree. You'll know it when you see it."

Margarita nodded to him, then headed into the complex, uncertain why this wondrous place filled her with dread.

It was all so beautiful — unthinkable that such a place could exist after everything that had happened. Margarita should have felt relief or hope or even happiness, but when she turned her attention inward she found her guard was still up. Feeling safe was so unnatural to her.

The sphere unfurled, revealing a lobby with bubbling fountains and manicured shrubs. If given the chance, they would choose this paradise over the humble home she'd built from the wreckage of that world that no longer was. If they left, where would that leave her?

She shrugged away her selfish thoughts as she explored the lobby. The sound of clinking glasses drew her attention to a dimly lit bar in the corner. A man in a crimson suit swiveled atop one of its chrome stools, waving to her.

Margarita approached warily. She'd always been suspicious of bars, preferring to drink in her own kitchen, surrounded by food and family. But a bar in this place seemed fitting. And even more fitting to find the reporter here. "Mr. Diaz?"

Vero was drinking pulque, white and filmy in his glass. "What a coincidence," he said between sips. "Are you settling in?"

She kissed the blade of his cheek. "Oh, I'm just visiting."

Vero nodded, but the narrowing of his look suggested doubt. Margarita eyed the stool beside him, but decided against taking it.

"I'm sorry about the Centro de Refugiados. It's a shame — I think a lot of people were expecting you to hold out longer."

Diaz's comment hooked into her heart like a barb. He was baiting her; she was sure of it. Why else would he say such a hurtful thing?

He took another drink of pulque, holding it in his mouth too long. She could tell by his wincing that he didn't like it. "It's easier if you don't look back."

Even immediately after the war, Margarita hadn't encountered many reporters. Were they all like this? So cynical?

Vero leaned to retrieve his suitcase. "I have something for you."

He handed her a sheet of what looked like glass but was as pliable as paper. Cerafilm. She had seen a billboard advertising it on the highway sometime before the war. "How do I —"

With a flick of his index finger, Vero activated the display. The words, "La Jardinera: The Gardener at the End of the World," appeared on the screen alongside a stylized dove, the logo for the *Daily Harbinger*. She skimmed the first few sentences of the Spanish version, immediately embarrassed by Diaz's use of words like "heroic" and "miraculous" to describe their world. She scrolled to the end of the article, intrigued by the commissioned portrait. *La Jardinera*. She searched the image for her likeness, finding echoes of the melancholy and hope of her days in the bleed of washed-out indigo and crimson. Yes, this image could have been her once. But the more she looked, the fainter the resemblance became. The painted woman was far younger, fairer, and prettier than she had ever been.

"You inspired a lot of people, Margarita. It's a shame the follow-up story will be such a disappointment." Vero gripped his knees as if he needed to steady himself. "But the truth is never convenient. Nothing lasts forever."

Margarita handed back the Cerafilm. "This is only temporary."

"Oh?" Vero leaned forward with interest. "Is it?"

"You doubt me?"

"I doubt *them*," Vero said, voice so low he was almost whispering. He tilted his head toward the agents in white milling about the lobby.

"How can you say that?" Margarita's tone was angrier than she'd intended. "They take care of us and this country the best they can. I'm grateful. You should be too."

For once, Vero had nothing to say. He shrunk into his chair like a scolded child, nursing the last of his pulque.

Among the terraces, the sweet fragrance of ripening sapotes and habanero chilis transported Margarita to a previous life: her and Roberto's parcel of maize, their avocado trees on tilled slopes, the chilis, poleo, and hoja santa she'd raised in her garden. This was the life that the hydrophage had turned to dust. Here it was, resurrected. But so much of it was still missing.

While admiring white flowers on a low-growing chaya shrub, she noticed a tree unlike any she had ever seen. Its pale, barrel-like trunk appeared buffed, smoothed into an arc of wide, flat boughs terminating in tiny leaves.

"Magnificent, isn't it?"

Too mesmerized by the foreign beauty to acknowledge Juaco's arrival, Margarita touched the smooth bark. "What is it?"

"A baobab, a transplant from west Africa. One of the last of its kind, recovered from the pyro zone." Juaco rounded the trunk, watching Margarita with amusement. "It's a resilient species, but without the joint intervention of the African Council and the United Nations Parliament, who knows what would have become of it."

Juaco gestured for her to sit at a curved glass bench surrounding the tree.

"You don't have to convince me of the good the United Nations brings to our country." Margarita sat beside the young man, adjusting her huipil. She had chosen a black garment patterned with vivid flowers. It suited the contradictions in her mood. "Their neutralizer packets kept us from thirst."

Juaco looked down at his hands, clasped in his lap. "I pray that one day we can take the helm and guide our people to prosperity without Green Zones or neutralizer packets or any more of these UN marvels."

"You worry you'll be eclipsed," Margarita ventured. "That they'll make you irrelevant." There was satisfaction in saying this out loud, even if she was talking about someone else.

Juaco looked down. "Sometimes I doubt we'll ever be strong enough to stand on our own two feet."

"Healing takes time, joven," Margarita said. "But you are young, and time moves differently for you."

He nodded, his affirmation colored with sorrow. "Before we were the People's Government, we were the Lobos. We were the hope and rage that unseated the Caudillo. But the country was in ruins, and we were just soldiers, not politicians. An angry mob can't build a government."

Margarita watched butterflies float overhead as she listened, their beauty a shield against the memories of dark days.

"We turned to the United Nations Parliament for aid. They brought their technology, their experts, their politicians. Helped us write our constitution. Helped us hunt down the last of the militias still loyal to the Caudillo." Juaco gestured to the structure that enveloped them. "They built *this*. And now they feed us. They protect us. As much as it shames me to say it, they rule us, because we need them to — because we lack."

Margarita smiled, an old assurance rising in her heart. "For now."

Juaco turned to her. "You were on your own out there. You managed with almost nothing. Meanwhile, I've been here in this comfortable shell. Most of the time I feel like I'm getting in the way." Juaco buried his face in hands. "I fought for this peace. I sacrificed everything to bring it about, but my heart is still at war. I look around at this paradise and all I feel is guilt. How do you do it, Margarita? How do you forget?"

"I don't forget." Margarita reached for Juaco's hand. "I focus on what is possible, on little things. That's what I learned from the revolution. Ordinary people are capable of anything. If they are willing to rebuild."

"I read the story that reporter wrote about you." Juaco leaned forward, resting his elbows on this thighs. "What happened to you, Margarita?"

She hesitated, but when she spoke her words emerged like an exhalation. A sigh of relief. "I was in one of the camps. They separated me from my family, but I did what I was told. It felt like an eternity, until your people came with the mark of the wolf. It was a bloody day. Many died on both sides."

Juaco tilted his head to her. "I am so sorry."

Margarita searched for the butterflies, but they had moved on. "I mourned them. The soldiers. The workers. Even our captors." She'd never told anyone of how she'd wept for the brutes who had stood over them, had pointed guns at them. Even that had seemed like a profound loss — of potential, of recovery. She didn't know what kind of person that made her, that she'd felt sorrow at this loss. But somehow she trusted Juaco with her confession.

"In war, who counts as friend or foe is not always clear." Juaco leaned forward until his eyes were level with hers. "You could have been relocated to one of the refugee camps, or even to the Green Zone if you accepted a post with the People's Government. How did you end up at the Centro de Refugiados?"

Margarita bowed her head. Quietly, she told Juaco about her lost family, the sórdidos she'd found in the valley, about Abuelo. "Just as you took up arms, so have I, in my own way. My people mustn't forget the sunrise — the light that always comes after the dark. And I won't have peace until I learn what this woman did to make our friend harm himself."

She could see bitterness flicker across Juaco's face. When they'd met at the Casa, he'd flared in anger when she'd said that she mourned him. Juaco stood, his posture once more that of a soldier. "I am not sure peace is possible anymore."

"Because of the Loba Roja?"

"Some call her Caudilla."

They stood and Margarita followed Juaco as he led them along the canal, toward another geometric structure. "You're the only person we know of who has seen her, spoken with her. By sharing what you know, you could help us stop her from sending us into another Desagüe or worse. I've arranged for you to speak to them, to the council. Will you help us?"

Margarita gripped Juaco's elbow as the steep path descended. "I will try my best."

At the entrance to the crystalline structure, two peacekeepers waited, their white armor glowing in the afternoon sun. But even in such bright light, Juaco's face darkened. "Margarita, I've buried things about my past. Terrible things. I used to think that forgetting was the best medicine."

Abuelo chose to remember.

Juaco shook his head as if to clear an unpleasant thought. "Never mind that. They're ready for you."

Margarita felt an irrational surge of fear as Juaco stepped away from her. "You're not coming?"

Juaco shook his head. "You'll do great without me."

Margarita followed the peacekeepers. She turned back as the men flanked her, so close she could feel the heat of their bodies. But Juaco had disappeared.

Inside the hexagonal structure, Margarita encountered a prismatic world of reflective walls and smooth-edged panes of aquamarine glass. LED projectors shone upon pearly surfaces, casting light like an ethereal gauze over the scene.

Positioned along a dais that encircled an inner platform, twelve UN peacekeepers were seated behind vitreous consoles. Released by her escorts, Margarita approached the platform, searching the peace-keepers' visors for a hint of their faces. The agents swiveled their heads toward her in unison, their movements almost mechanical. The one in front of her drew a circle in the air, their fingers trailing cerulean light on an invisible display. Following this gesture, a table and chairs of printed glass rose up from a hidden compartment in the platform. Margarita waited for instructions, but her hosts were silent.

She sat down. The chair felt cold on her back.

"Welcome," one of the peacekeepers said, the mechanical voice revealing little about the speaker behind it.

Margarita put on a smile, relieved that the silence was broken, if nothing else.

"Are you pleased with your accommodations, Señora Urbina?" The peacekeeper to her right asked, the iridescent fabric of their cape sparkling as they spoke.

Margarita squinted — the room seemed to be getting brighter, or maybe her eyes needed more time to adjust. "We are very grateful."

"We understand that you have had dealings with a person of interest to us," said a voice behind her. A peacekeeper took the seat across from her. "Is that so?"

Margarita nodded, detecting the glimmer of an iris behind their visor. This mirage of an eye reassured her that her host was human.

"Tell us."

"A woman who called herself Aleja." The intensity of the silence in the chamber did nothing to conceal the nerves in Margarita's voice. She wondered what technology was behind such profound quiet.

"She said she was with the People's —"

"*She* is not the person of interest to us."

Goosebumps rose on the back of her arms. "I don't understand."

The central peacekeeper stood. At their full height, they towered over her. Margarita shrank back.

"When you spoke to Joaquín you mentioned another."

"Abuelo," Margarita squinted, certain now that the lights were getting brighter, the air colder by the minute.

"You told Joaquín this Abuelo was 'important' to you. How important?"

"What does this have to do with —"

They opened their palms toward the ceiling, a gesture which amplified the projectors' lumens, transforming the agent before her into a seraphic figure, its cape unfurling into what looked like six wings.

"Was this 'Abuelo' your lover?"

"Excuse me?" Margarita shielded her eyes with her hand. She started to get up, but gloved hands held her in place. Then with a snap, ice-cold restraints coiled around her legs and hands. For a moment, she lost all sense of time, thrust back to her days at the labor camp in Flores. Days of unspeakable pain and dehumanization at the hands of tormentors who reveled in her suffering. Somehow, this was worse. The soldiers in Flores had been men. But the ones holding her now were like the angels that her mother had feared upon her conversion. Those monstrosities wreathed in white fire, serving a God more vengeful than the volcano or the rainmaker to whom she gave ofrendas.

Mother was right to fear them.

"You will not be harmed if you cooperate," they said.

"My feelings are a private matter," Margarita managed, her gaze settling on the still-luminous agent. Juaco knew they were interested in Abuelo. In that knowledge, Margarita felt the sting of betrayal. He had sent her in here without warning. "But the answer is no."

"Good," a voice said from the raised dais. "Now tell us about this woman."

Margarita closed her eyes, searching her memory for everything she could recall about Aleja. Her long walks with Abuelo in the dusty hills. Her overuse of makeup, perhaps as a disguise. Her musings about the ancient Maya and a creature of myth, a wolf that carries the dead to the underworld. The day Margarita found Abuelo's desiccated corpse in the bunker. She told them all of it. They recorded her words, scanning her voice and biosigns for evidence that she was lying.

After what seemed like hours of detailed recollection, Margarita found the courage to ask, "May I go now?"

"Soon," the agent said. Their fingers danced over shimmering screens as they spoke. "You must understand. This Aleja has become a great threat to the Yucatán and beyond. We had to be certain."

Margarita fidgeted in her chair, her body aching from the restraints. "Certain about what?"

"That you are not an accomplice."

Five days later, she met Juaco at the baobab tree. He had slipped an official letter under her door, on letterhead from the People's Government, informing her that her house arrest was over and that all pending charges had been dropped. He was there at the bench with a tray holding two steaming biofilm cups. He rested the tray on the bench, standing up to greet her, but before he had a chance to utter a word, she slapped him.

"I deserve that," Juaco said, rubbing his cheek.

In her retaliation, Margarita was both satisfied and contrite. "You should have warned me."

"That would have been treason."

Margarita turned away from him, scowling.

Juaco fetched the tray from the bench, as the jacanas started to sing. She took a cleansing breath and regarded him thoughtfully, searching his face for signs of malice. She was sure that her previous impression of him was not wrong. He'd been following orders. He had never given his heart to cruelty and deception. But she could never entirely trust him.

"And what is that?" she asked, intrigued by a smoky aroma wafting from the tray. "Atonement?"

"We grow the beans here," he said warmly, handing her a cup.

She took a sip, savoring the rich aroma and body of the coffee, noting a hint of something she had almost forgotten. "That's roasted corn, isn't it? I haven't had that since … How did you know?"

"I ordered it special for you." Juaco blew on his cup to cool it down. "There were some Ladinos and Tzetlales in my unit. They preferred their coffee this way. Said that corn is what their bones are made of."

She pressed her eyes shut, savoring the sweet notes of maize on her tongue. "Thank you."

"The United Nations Parliament and the People's Government would like to keep you around for another week or so as they verify the intel you provided. Until then, you and your people are free to roam as you please."

Juaco watched an oriole perched on a young baobab branch. When he turned back to her, he nodded toward her cup. "There's more where that came from."

Margarita smiled, still lost in the earthy taste and silky texture of the coffee.

Tucking his hands in his pockets, Juaco stood. "Look, I know I've violated your trust."

Margarita gulped down the last of her coffee and paced to the chaya at the edge of the baobab clearing.

"I want to earn it back." Juaco's voice was suddenly tight. "Please, I know you can never forget what I've done —"

Kneeling by the chaya shrub, Margarita combed through its woody stalks, searching for weeds. It was something she'd done on her farm, the meticulousness of it calming her. "Earlier you said forgetting might be the best medicine." She tugged at a few pale strands of crab-grass, pulling where the base touched the soil to get at the root, the way Mother had taught her. "I can't say I agree. I cherish the pain. It's all I have left of the people I lost and the woman I once was. Who would I be if I forgot those things?"

Juaco frowned. "It's easier to be someone else than to face what you lost."

Margarita harvested one of the chaya leaves, pinching it off to encourage new growth. "A plant like this one will survive my harvest-ing, just as it might survive droughts or flooding or fires or diseases." She eyed the clusters of white blossoms. "Even after all that it still finds a way to bloom. Not by forgetting what it has been through, but by building on it."

Juaco shook his head, his voice retreating to a whimper. "I've done terrible things, Doña. My roots are rotten."

She peered at him over the flowers. "God gives even the worst of his children second chances."

Above the sphere, clouds clotted the sky in a slate-hued mosaic. After her ordeal with the UN agents, Margarita found the dim light comfort-ing. She selected a bushel of plantains for molotes she would share with Ismael and Ximena and the other sórdidos. Seeking a new route back to the residence, Margarita ventured to the edge of the great sphere, leaving the orchard and the lapping waters of the canal behind.

Arriving at a cargo bay, she watched freight drones haul crates of supplies, and wheeled delivery drones transfer them to modular containers.

In the warehouse, massive unidentifiable parts were printed and assembled by tentacled drones. To her they looked like jellyfish. She was startled when a massive hauler drone whizzed by, its wheels slick with the familiar clay of her world beyond this one. She studied the cargo in the bed of the driverless hauler, a gigantic shape wrapped in canvas tarp to protect it from the rains. Water pooling in the folds of tarp, streaming off the hauler, reminded her of her Casa in the valley, defenseless in the water's path. Her breath caught in her throat as she imagined the house buckling under the water's weight. No one was there to witness it.

As another hauler passed, the canvas cloak in the bed came loose and it ballooned like a sail, revealing a plastichrome exoskeleton. It must have been two storeys tall. Beyond the ivory hued meshwork of plates and cabling, a crown of spines pulsed with green light.

It's looking at me.

"This is a restricted area!"

A pair of white-armored UN peacekeepers appeared from behind her. She could not read their expressions, but the clip of their movements suggested urgency. What exactly had she seen?

"I lost my way," Margarita offered, nodding to her gathered plantains. Flores had taught her that feigned ignorance could sometimes save a life. "I'm bringing these back to my habitación to make fritters. I can make extra if —"

Do they even eat?

The peacekeepers replied in unison. "We will escort you."

Later in her kitchen, as she peeled the plantains, she tried to shut out images of gore splattered over the snowy dunes of Siberia. Images from the Novemberists' failed revolution against the theocracy that the Russian Federation had become. To imagine that evil machinery on her own continent was too much for her to bear. Margarita diced the golden flesh of the plantains into starchy coins. Tossing them into a wooden bowl, she tried not to see in those rounded shapes pairs of celadon eyes.

The command tower was a glass platform high above the sphere's printed structures. As Juaco led Margarita into the attached amphitheater, she tried not to look through the tower's transparent floor. Instead, she fixed her gaze to the rain-streaked sphere, to the muddied valley beyond. Her fear of heights did nothing to mask her trepidation over Juaco's intentions, why he'd brought her here. She'd agreed to meet him, but she'd never trust him again.

"I never wanted you to suffer."

Juaco steered her into the heart of the amphitheater and they stood together, surrounded by twelve consoles manned by the UN's agents. Despite herself, she was shaking, finding too much of her previous interrogation in this new scene.

An agent to her right stirred and a mechanical voice emanated from behind their smooth visor. *"The Loba Roja cannot be contained by conventional measures."*

"Subterfuge was necessary to recreate past events and triangulate the terrorist's objectives," the agent to her left said.

Margarita eyed the apostolic figures, wary of their subtle movements. "If you're peacekeepers, why do you bring weapons to our land?"

"Counter-terrorism measures. Courtesy of Her Excellency the UN Premier."

Margarita flinched, trying to forget the terrifying flicker of their eyes.

"We are at war, Margarita," Juaco reminded her.

"There must be another way," Margarita said, her gaze rounding to each peacekeeper.

"We have it under control," Juaco said. "Now it's time we repay you for your cooperation."

Margarita waved a hand dismissively at the idea of "payment." She didn't want anything from Juaco, and especially not from these white devils.

"Give whatever you're offering to my people."

Juaco shook his head. "This gift is for you. It will set you free."

With a crackle of static, the sky vanished and the sphere around them transformed into a musty bunker. In the projected image, Abuelo slouched in a chair. His posture was not unlike how he'd sometimes sat in the sala, when he'd wanted to be left alone. A familiar woman stood over him, cigar in hand.

"Do you feel it, the pull of the past?"

Without her wig and the prosthetics she had used to cover her burns, the bald woman Margarita once knew as Aleja looked far more sinister. White smoke roped out of her mouth, coiling above her midnight eyes.

Juaco squeezed her wrist, suddenly giddy. Something about his smile unsettled her.

"Gonzalo Ocasio Reyes," said Abuelo. Margarita shook her head. No — it was the voice of someone else coming through him. That other person who slumbered within him. She could feel Juaco's eyes on her, urging her to the inevitable conclusion. Margarita shook her head again.

"I was supposed to forget!"

The sphere reverberated with screams as his body shriveled before her eyes. Her own screams.

"Your blood feeds Buluc Chabtan. We will need his blessing for the war that is to come."

Margarita didn't hear the Loba as she whispered to Abuelo's dried corpse. She had already found her way out of the amphitheater, through the hall, into the lift. With unsteady fingers she pressed the button for the ground floor again and again. As the lift lurched into motion, her world spiraled.

The door had scarcely opened when Margarita retched, her body rebelling against incomprehensible cruelty. Her heart was sick for Abuelo, for the devastation of how he'd been taken, finally, to God. But also for the cruelty he had inflicted on so many souls, including her Roberto and her children and all of the sórdidos. Weeping, Margarita stumbled through the orchards, nauseated by the ceiba blossoms which reeked of blood.

At the baobab tree, she prayed. She pleaded to her Lady of Guadalupe to bring peace to a troubled world. She presented an offering for the mountains, as those of the original word, those batzil'op, might have done.

Mother, I haven't forgotten how to be grateful.

The sound of footsteps told her she was not alone.

"I thought you would be happy." Juaco's voice was coarse with anger. "He was a monster. He deserved to burn."

Margarita turned to face the young man. The eyes that met hers were dark and sunken. "*Mijo,* you confuse revenge for justice."

The soldier gritted his teeth, towering over her. "He killed your family!" he bellowed, as if somehow she had forgotten. Margarita closed her eyes as the certainty rose within her. The soldier yearned to grieve, but the world had not yet let him.

"I take no pleasure in watching anyone be killed," Margarita said as she turned to look at Juaco. "There is no beauty or sanity in war."

Juaco sank to the bench, running a hand over his face.

"I weep for *him* as much as I weep for anyone else." Margarita lifted herself from her vigil and sat beside him. "God gave him a second chance."

"A second chance," Juaco repeated, as if to himself. "That's what you said to the reporter. The Casa was your second chance to have a family. But how can you forgive? How can you forget what he took from us?"

"No, joven. Haven't you been listening?" Margarita said, the ferocity of her glare hardening her voice. "I don't forget. We can't grow by running away from the past or burying it. We must remember it all, no matter how painful. Yes, I feel betrayed. I feel angry. But I refuse to be consumed by hatred. If I did that, I would never have survived this war."

Juaco slumped, his hands limp in his lap.

Margarita rose from the bench. "It's time for us to go home."

His eyes widened with alarm. "To the Centro de Refugiados? But it's gone ... washed away."

"Then we'll rebuild, as we always have," Margarita said with a smile. "War is a circle, Juaco. These angels mean to use the evil sleeping in those haulers. The war they will bring will undo everything you've built here. And after the last shots are fired, they will abandon us. I won't wait for the cycle to start over. I'd rather live in the dirt."

floración | flourishing

"For centuries we languished while they flourished. Marionettes on the end of their strings. Spain. America. China. We must seize the strings from their prying hands to steer our own destiny. We will never be free until we step out of the shadows of our barbaric past."

Gonzalo Ocasio Reyes, *Inaugural Address to the National Assembly*

"To those rendered destitute by this petty war of East and West. To those left out of their Parliamentary vision — we offer you a seat at *our* table. We are the answer to this false peace. The mantra of 'One World' we answer with a resounding *No!*"

Silicon Fox (suspected alias), "Stateless: A Manifesto," excerpted from *How an unlikely alliance of Cryptobarons, Biotech Smugglers, & Augscape Hackers formed the Table*. United Nations University Library, Geneva.

V ero Diaz was wary of the broad-leafed ceibas on either side of the muddy track. As a child in Puerto Rico, his grandfather had told him that ceiba roots were the braids of hexed kings trailing them as they plunged to the underworld in a slow katabasis.
"Distance to contact is 100 meters."

His SEAX bobbed as it evaded sinewy lianas and fugitive creepers. Sunlight trickled down through the thick canopy, dappling the chrome sphere of its body with patches of shadow.

Vero squashed a mosquito on his forehead. "How is that possible? There's nothing here but snakes and bugs."

And howler monkeys. The creatures roared unseen in the boughs above him, their voices more canine than simian. The sound raised the hair on his arms, but Vero ventured deeper into the Maya forest, that stubborn swatch of wilderness that the hydrophage failed to snuff out. As he breathed in the humid air, he wondered what timeless sorcery had protected this oasis in the Caudillo's desert.

What if Nuwairah is right? What if I'm being set up?

His Editor-in-Chief had warned him of the danger. The possibility that he might be taken hostage chilled him, but he weighed the risk against the reward. If successful, he would be the first reporter to interview this mysterious Caudilla since her infamous broadcast.

Something crunched beneath his boot. Not a twig. Something metallic. Before he could study the device, the forest shifted around him. A series of hidden projectors deactivated the illusion of dense jungle before him.

There you are.

A pyramid of vermillion-painted stone jutted up from a newly-revealed clearing. Four gigantic ceibas formed a ring around its base. Their roots netted into a rhizomatic walkway that brought him to the steps of a structure that rivaled the Great Jaguar Temple in Yax Mutul.

"Well, SEAX," Vero whispered, catching a glimpse of his gray-streaked hair in the orb's reticulating glass eye. "It was nice knowing you."

"I don't understand your query, sir. Please restate your request."

"Never mind," Vero sighed, steeling himself for the ascent. On account of the humid air and his bad knees, each step was more difficult than the last. As he pushed upward, Vero rehearsed his questions and the many what-if-things-go-south scenarios he had imagined prior to embarking on what Nuwairah had called "a chance to cash in on his life insurance policy."

Each adobe lintel brimmed with glyphs brightened by indigo and gold pigments. Feathered serpents. Monkey deities. Bipedal canines bearing torches. They were not entirely unlike Taíno petroglyphs he had seen in the Caribbean; zoomorphic shapes scrawled onto stones near the waterfalls and mountain rivers he'd played in as a child. His grandfather had nurtured this interest, driving him to the archaeological parks and hidden places on the island where the remnants of their extinct civilization endured. Abey was so disappointed when Vero decided to major in journalism instead of archaeology at university. But Vero had always preferred to tell stories of the living rather than exhume those of the dead.

He stopped to drink water from his flask, counting the remaining steps to the summit. From this height, the expanse of the forest was staggering and absolute, a sea of lush green that at any moment might drown him.

"*You have arrived at your destination,*" his SEAX reported.

Vero studied the thick vegetation, shivering as he recalled a dream he'd had the night prior. Abey in a forest like this one. Whispering to him in the dead language of the Taíno. Vero naked and trembling, streaked with red paint, or was it blood? Where his navel should have been, there was nothing. When he looked up at Abey, his grandfather had transformed into a bone-white monolith. One of the dreaming stones. Vero had screamed as the cemí's carved mouth spoke, as the craters of its eyes turned to him.

I'm not dreaming.

Something in the jungle's understory moved. Not one, but two shapes. Lithe and quick. The ferns undulated with their approach. Was this another technological feint? A snarl, guttural and wet, evaporated his fantasy of safety.

106

"*Unknown biosigns detected.*" The spherical shell of the SEAX rotated as it searched for the interlopers.

"Show yourself!" Vero shouted. Though he'd tried to project confidence, his voice cracked as it echoed through the forest.

As if summoned, two creatures emerged from the forest, loping up the stairs to greet him. Their brown coats were tinged unnaturally scarlet. Moving with preternatural speed and precision, they leapt with their pricked ears and gleaming incisors on full display, rushing past him to block his path to the final step of the pyramid. These were no dogs. They were more like wolves or jackals, only larger, somehow altered.

"Heel!" A resonant alto sounded from behind the slobbering lupines. They parted from his path and sat, looking as benign as house pets.

"Hunahpu and Xbalanque," the voice said. "A gift from the Garuda, bioengineered for my protection … or assassination. I have yet to determine which."

A circular dais rose from a hidden compartment atop the pyramid, revealing a figure reclined in a throne carved from limestone, canine visages bursting from its armrests. Vero swallowed hard as he took stock of the woman before him. Her face mottled with burns. Her nose like a cloven hoof jutting from painted whorls of red and black. A beaded necklace of jade teeth draped her collarbone. A wolf appeared to leap from her bare sternum, inked to the scarred skin that stretched over her missing breasts. The simple black hoodie and stained jeans she wore seemed a mockery of the exquisite symbolism of this place, and the headdress of quetzal feathers that adorned her clean-shaven scalp.

Vero found his voice. "So the rumors are true — you *are* seeking an alliance with the Table."

The Loba Roja extended her arms in the direction of her strange pets. "Accepting these scientific curiosities into my fold is hardly proof of that. I have declined their offer for now."

She leaned forward, her obsidian earrings somehow not as black as her eyes. "But you've not come to talk about pirates, have you?"

"No, I haven't," Vero stammered before he could catch his breath.

"K'ulaj," she said in a language he did not recognize. "Welcome to Tulan, a place of myth once forgotten, now remembered."

Vero thought to bow, but decided against it. "I have come to hear your story."

Behind her, the dark shapes of men climbed the pyramid, their bronze bodies glistening with sweat and red paint. Their faces were concealed by canid masks that he feared might howl as they lifted their obsidian spears.

"Good," the Loba said, laughing bitterly. "I was beginning to believe that you were a spy for the United Nations Parliament." Her guards pointed their black polearms at his neck. Beams of red light issued from the tips of the weapons. "My wayob will know if you are true."

Some kind of scanner?

"He poses no danger, my Tepew," one of the wolf-men said, bowing his head.

"You may leave us." She nodded to her panting wolves. "The twins will provide sufficient protection."

As her wayob descended the pyramid, the Loba gestured to a stool carved from dark jade opposite her throne. Vero sat, his SEAX keeping sufficient distance to capture images of the conversation.

"Would you permit me to record our session?"

"So that you can distort my words through editorial trickery?" The Loba replied, flashing teeth that looked like they had been filed.

Vero straightened on the stool. "You have no reason to trust me. But I'm different from the others. I don't use algos to write my stories. I'm as real as it gets. And I'm here to help bring your story to the world — to let your truth speak."

The Loba's eyes narrowed with delight. "Well, in that case, let the truth speak. Broadcast this conversation live for all to see. No enhancements, no filtering, no sound bites."

Vero imagined the wolves could smell his terror. A live broadcast meant that everything he said was subject to scrutiny. He hadn't been this nervous since he interviewed the Tsarina.

"Agreed. SEAX, initiate broadcast."

"*We are live,*" the SEAX informed him, the myriad lenses of its camera array glinting like the compound eyes of insects.

Vero fidgeted in his seat, suddenly reminded that he was interviewing the most dangerous woman in the Americas. After taking a moment for composure, the words flowed from him, some scripted, some improvised.

"Good afternoon, this is Vero Diaz of the *Daily Harbinger*, reporting live from an undisclosed location in the Yucatán. I am not here against my will, nor am I being held prisoner. I come seeking the truth."

The SEAX panned to the Loba Roja, whose hands were folded neatly in her lap.

"Now, if you'll kindly introduce yourself, for the record."

In her throne, she exuded a startling calm. "I am many. But if you must call me something it is the Loba Roja, le kiäqa utiw, the Red Queen of New Mayapán, liberator of those who yearn to be free from the yoke of Sino-Euro civilization. I am the voice of those so oppressed, those who have so internalized their own conquest that they stand ready to die for the very oppressors who have for half a millennium wrought only chaos and death on our lands."

This Caudilla is certainly different from the last one.

"You will soon understand," the Loba said, crossing her legs, "that you have been chosen. I chose you because your story is not as different from mine as you might think. In fact, *you* might have become me if circumstances were different."

This isn't supposed to be about me.

109

Vero shifted in his seat. "It's difficult to imagine how anyone could become like you. But none of us know your story, the path that led you to become the Loba Roja."

The Loba grinned, an expression he'd previously seen on the muzzles of her mutant pets. "Some paths choose us."

"And how did this path find you?" Vero met her smoldering glare. "Where did it begin?" He held the question up as bait, praying she would take it.

The Loba smiled and turned to the SEAX floating above them. "It starts with my father. He was one of those opportunistic Ladinos who moved to the city from the countryside at a young age. He traded his machete for a briefcase, his saco for a suit and tie, his Yucatec for perfect Spanish. But when he went to university, he turned away from the world of business to study the past he left behind, the world of the Maya he'd forgotten."

"And your mother?"

"Xquic. In this tongue, her name was something like Waning Moon. A K'iche' speaking girl from the highland villages. Father, then an anthropologist-in-training, came to her sierra hoping to study our Deer Dance. He met Waning Moon by the fire on the eve of the harvest. And so it was that he came to love what she represented but failed to understand who she truly was."

"And who was she, really?"

"An operative appointed by a secret council of Maya, Lacandon, Tzeltal, Tzotzil, K'iche, Kaqchikel, and Ixil elders." Her jade necklace clinked as she gesticulated. "Sent to infiltrate the government that excluded and oppressed them."

Vero thumbed his chin, feeling doubt in the trace of stubble there. The Loba could have been describing herself. Or some fabricated personal mythology. "So your father knew nothing of this?"

The Loba shook her head. "He underestimated her. In this same way, he underestimated me. But we were there at the political meetings, when the Caudillo ran for office, using my father and his Maya wife as props at campaign rallies in the villages. He needed indio votes to win."

"How did your father turn from the academy to politics?"

"When Androvirus swept through the world, climate change had so ravaged supply chains that only rich nations had access to vaccines. Those willing to take a side in the cold war might get access from China or America. The National Assembly failed to act. My father and his archaeologist mentor saw this as an opportunity. Their answer was to create a new political party built on nativism and isolationism, citing the grandeur of Maya civilization as proof of this nation's capacity for independence."

"This archaeologist you refer to is the late President Gonzalo Ocasio Reyes?"

"Yes, he was my father's mentor at university. They decided Gonzalo would be the face of the party, not my father. They figured a light-skinned mestizo who claimed to fight for the indios would be less threatening. The grift resulted in a landslide victory."

"Did your father ever suspect that the Caudillo was using him?"

"My mother did, but he never listened to her, even after the Caudillo's first address to the Assembly, when he reversed course on the Maya, calling for the nation to forget its 'barbaric' past."

Vero squinted as the sun peeked out from the clouds, gilding the roof comb atop the pyramid. "Was your father involved with the development of the hydrophage?"

"Yes." The Loba drew in a breath. "Gonzalo and Hector worked with a Chinese firm to make good on their campaign promise to stop the advance of the dry corridor along the Sierra Madre. The firm deployed a biochemical agent that they hoped might improve hydraulic retention. But the experiments failed. Instead of healing the land, the chemical agent proved to be hydrophobic, exacerbating the problem further."

"So the hydrophage was initially devised to heal the land rather than harm it?"

The Loba gestured to the twin lupines, whose heads swiveled in response. "Many things are not faithful to their origins."

The sun moved behind the comb, and its shadow enveloped them. Now wreathed in darkness, the red ink of the Loba's tattoos seemed more vibrant. "When dissent erupted, Gonzalo's reprisal was brutal. He threw students and political opponents into prisons, framing them as Chinese or American spies. For my father, that was the line in the sand.

"Thus the Lobos were born. They struck from the wilderness using guerilla tactics. But Gonzalo was crueler than we could have imagined. He repurposed the failed hydraulic tech into a climate weapon, striking at the heart of the Indigenous communities where the Lobos hid.

"He appeared on television shortly after, announcing that the indios were aiding and abetting terrorists working with the Americans and the Chinese to end the republic. Then came the second purge, the internment camps, the severing of telecom networks, and the erasure of anyone that opposed him from history."

"And that's when he came for your family?"

"Yes." The Loba nodded. "In those final days, Gonzalo's behavior became erratic, paranoid even. He gave execution orders for his relatives, fearful of would-be rivals or successors. And then he dissolved the National Assembly, ending the Republic."

"Can you confirm the rumors that Gonzalo was unvaccinated?"

The Loba reclined in her throne. "He told us once, over cognac, that he would rather slit his wrists than inject himself with a drug formulated by American scientists and Chinese computers."

Now for the hard questions.

Vero tapped his foot on the stone floor. "Were you there when your father was executed?"

Her voice softened for the first time. "My father hid my mother and I in a safehouse in the sierra. On the eve of the Lobos' assault on the capital, father came to check on us but Gonzalo and his macheteros had followed."

The Loba traced the tattoos that marked her scarred chest. "They did this to me and my mother, and then killed my father, making us watch as he took his final breath." The Loba's hands clenched into fists. "He set the place ablaze, leaving us to burn. But I remain before you now because his men mistook me for dead."

The Caudillo created her.

"No one deserves to suffer like that." Vero regretted his words instantly, certain that she would spit on his pity.

The SEAX repositioned itself for an over-the-shoulder shot.

"But their sacrifice was not in vain, wouldn't you say? The rebels won and the Reyes regime fell."

The Loba did not reply, her fingers drumming on her armrests.

As if to fill what felt like an expansive silence, Vero leaned forward. "Many wonder why you didn't make your survival public, why you didn't come forward in the early years of the People's Government. You would have had the support of your father's coalitions. You could have easily been elected as the new President."

The Loba tilted her head, highlighting the brilliant green of the quetzal feathers in her headdress. "That would only lead to history repeating itself. You see, Gonzalo was right about one thing. The ones who broke the world should not be entrusted with its repair."

"You refer to the United Nations Parliament?"

It had been years since he'd left, but Vero remembered the fear in Alonsito's face as the "aliens" crested the mountain. How he'd decided on the spot to go with the UN agents had always puzzled him. But he was certain staying would have been worse.

Turning to one of the wolves, the Loba steepled her hands and cast Vero a sidelong glance. Her look pierced him, exposed him.

"In the eleventh hour of the conflict, my father made a deal with them to rebuild our government and repair the land damaged by the hydrophage in exchange for weapons and supplies."

"A partnership which bore fruit, wouldn't you agree?" Vero indicated to the lush greenery around him. "My sources tell me precipitation has increased beyond pre-hydrophage levels."

The Loba laughed, her face contorting into a scowl. "Mr. Diaz, you disappoint me."

"I'm reporting the facts."

"Facts." The Loba raised a finger to the sky. "Lies refurbished as truths. Tell me, Mr. Diaz, are you not the author of an exposé that casts doubt on the effectiveness of Gonggong™, the chemical cocktail that was dispensed on our land to neutralize the hydrophage?"

Vero coughed. "I did write that piece but the context was —"

The Loba's fingers traced glyphs in the air that faded as swiftly as they appeared, projected by unseen displays. His article appeared in a translucent blue font. "A growing number of scientists are casting doubt on the efficacy of Gonggong™ to reverse desertification due to the residual toxicity that results from prolonged application, preventing plants from rooting and resulting in topsoil drift."

Vero signaled for the SEAX to come closer, watching in its reflection as wrinkles carved doubt into his face. "What are you implying?"

"As you so eloquently put it, I only wonder if 'profit motives' have influenced the work of the engineers behind this neutralizer agent? Where there is profit, politics follow. In this case, a politics of dependency. In this era, conquest wears many faces."

Vero tugged at his collar. "Are you alleging that the UN Parliament have been knowingly administering an ineffectual solution to the climate disaster here?"

"Come on, Mr. Diaz, you know what I am saying." The Loba shook her head with disgust. "You're just afraid to say it out loud with everyone watching."

114

Demons can take the shape of angels, mother used to say.

"You think the climate repair drones were poisoning the land deliberately, promising a restoration they knew would never come, so your country would continue to remain dependent on the UN economically and politically. Possibly even to cast themselves as saviors in the public eye."

"Precisely."

Vero slumped in his chair. "A bold idea. But what makes this different than any other conspiracy theory?"

"Like the one that suggests the Androvirus was created in a lab, unleashed by radical feminist Marxists to unseat men from global power?"

"A theory that was easily disproved with evidence. It was never a 'man's' virus in the first place, the gender disparity was a result of diagnostic bias. Few regarded women's claims of cognitive decline seriously. Anyway, scientists have overwhelming evidence that the retrovirus is of an ancient origin. It was waiting in the permafrost. The planet punished us for letting it burn."

"So you would defend them, the ones who set the world ablaze?"

My position is irrelevant.

Vero shifted, gesturing to his SEAX and sending it away again. As a journalist he wasn't used to having the frame repeatedly turn to him. He was used to controlling his own story.

"What evidence do you have to support these allegations against the UN? Your country is green again after months of rain. If the neutralizer agent was a ruse, how do you explain that? How do you explain the restoration of your land?"

The Loba rose from her throne, positioning herself to address the SEAX directly. "The fanged Chaak brought back the rains, and through me, the world that was lost was rekindled with fire that does not burn."

"Many will find what you're saying hard to believe."

"Belief is not necessary." The Loba stepped toward him as a jade brazier ascended from an unseen chamber below. "Do you think it a coincidence that the rains followed my emergence, the day the Caudillo met his end?"

Vero had seen the broadcast and the desiccated husk that remained at the end of it. But that hadn't been the most troubling thing about the video. That had been the look on the Loba's face as the Caudillo had withered. The same look she wore now.

"It would seem so," Vero said, watching as the Loba lit a fire in the brazier.

"Then you are mistaken." The Loba tended to the flames, the musky fragrance of copal resins a haze rising from the stones. "The One-Worlders you bow to have sought me out for months. Not to sue for peace, but because they know I am in possession of a cache of weapons left behind by the late Caudillo — weapons they fear I will use against their beloved seats of power."

The Loba filled a clay bowl with water from a decanter and set it atop the flame. "Earlier you were surprised to learn that the hydrophage was originally designed to rejuvenate rather than harm. You must remember, Mr. Diaz, we Maya have always been terraform-ers." She pulled out a vial from her pocket, releasing a drop of rusty liquid into the bowl. "My ancestors were not noble savages who lived and died in passive harmony with our surroundings. We were architects — hydraulic visionaries who bent seas and rivers and lakes to our will."

Vero flicked his hand, a signal the SEAX recognized, and it moved in for a close-up of the brazier.

"I consulted our chuchqajaw and divined what was necessary to save our lands," the Loba said, peering into the bowl billowing with a copal-scented cloud. "I ordered that the hydrophage be detonated at sea."

Vero held his breath as the cloud moistened his cheeks.

116

The Loba lifted the empty bowl. "It was I, not that cabal of usurpers clad in white, who resurrected the Yucatán."

Vero turned to face the SEAX. "You heard it here first: the Loba Roja claiming responsibility for the rehydration of the Yucatán, alleging foul play on the part of the UN. But now I have a personal question." Vero eyed the brazier as it trailed copal smoke. "Do you feel any remorse for what you did to Gonzalo?"

The Loba sank back into her throne, folding her arms in her lap. "If you think his death was the satisfaction of some personal vendetta, you are gravely mistaken. By killing him, I exorcise the colonizer's ghost from our consciousness. I deliver us from a lineage of macho fools — Simón Bolívar, Porfirio Díaz, Rios Mont, Gonzalo Ocasio Reyes — who could never face the truth. Conquest can never be undone through Iberian thinking."

In that moment, the sun aligned with a slit in the roof comb, and the Loba rose from her throne, arms reaching out, as light radiated behind her like the fiery petals of a Xukul Nict. "I am the seed that will sprout a new future, and my subjects are the moisture that will nourish my tree of apostasy, until my boughs shatter the sky into the stars beyond."

The last of the copal vapor coiled before her tenebrous eyes. Watching her, Vero's breath caught in his throat. She was playing to the audience, delivering hope to some and fear to others.

"We are tomorrow's waters, a hydraulic dream of liberation. Like a wave we rise up to crash upon the shores of yesterday. And indeed some waves are great enough to unmake the shore entirely. *That* is what I intend to become."

Vero closed his eyes briefly, but a moment was all he needed to remember the way Teddy redrew the shorelines of his beloved home, remade the beaches. Would the Loba Roja be another Teddy? She could be a destruction unlike any before her. The thought horrified and excited him. Vero studied the sovereign, no longer so threatened, even as shafts of sunlight elevated her into something like a solar deity.

When the sun slipped behind the comb once again, Vero stood, his legs shaking. Alerted to his slightest movements, the Loba's wolves bolted into action. They prowled, one on either side of him, an eerie sapience written in their gazes.

"And what of peace?" he whispered.

"If peace is to be defined on their terms …" The Loba knelt as her wolves approached, cautiously sniffing the air around her. "Then no."

"What are your terms?"

"You already know."

"Do I?"

"You know the gardener at the end of this world," the Loba said, adding wood to the brazier. "The valley's caretaker."

Vero frowned. "Señora Urbina?"

"Yes," The Loba said. "She frames our future, if we share in her courage."

"I don't understand." Vero's head spun. From what he'd heard in the Green Zone, from people in the valley, he'd expected ruthlessness from the Loba. He'd anticipated violence. But this was a surprise.

"I am merely a shaper," she said, voice suddenly soft. "From the Rio Grijalva to the Rio Ulua. From Xcalumkín to the pine forests of the Sierra Madre, the world that was once Maya red shall be reshaped by my hand, but for what comes after, we must look to Doña Margarita. That is what it means to rule from below."

Vero ran his fingers through his hair. His hand came away wet with sweat and humidity. When he spoke again the words that emerged didn't sound like his own. "You won't treat with the United Nations Parliament, not even to broker a peace?"

"Is that why you have come?" The Loba studied him intently, tongues of flame curling before her eyes. "To broker their peace? You need look no further than the Treaty of Beijing to see that their version of peace is paper conquest."

She turned from the brazier, her wolves following close behind. "True peace will come when the last of the colonizers have vanished and when the lingering ghosts of their presence, their corrupted frames of republics and democracies and parliaments have been excised from our consciousness. We were once the apex of civilization in these lands, and so we shall be again a beacon of inspiration for the world and those countless others that still slave under the yoke of Sino-Euro civilization."

The Loba's voice grew cold. "But you never answered me. Have you come on their behalf?"

Shit.

Vero retreated cautiously, signaling to the SEAX to pan out. If he was going to die, he wanted the world to know what happened to him — what this Loba Roja was capable of. The wolves were already circling him, growling, "Of course not. I —"

"Tepew." Vero recognized the voice of her wayob, as he reached the pyramid's apex.

The Loba turned to Vero with a wry smile. "Did you know that the gods had no anuses? That they could feast on scent alone?"

The wayob approached their Tepew, their obsidian pikes and wolf-like masks an otherworldly blur of black and red, disrupted by something pale in their midst. Four newcomers, clad in white.

Aliens. Here.

He had been outmaneuvered in a game of three-dimensional chess. Soon he would be dead, another journalist assassinated in this hopeless age.

The Loba tilted her head in the direction of the prisoners, their armors glittering. "My wayob — my were-men — possess the gift of scent. Like Hunahpu and Xbalanque they can smell vermin coming from twenty kilometers away."

"I'm not with them!" Vero shouted, aware of how cowardly he must have sounded. He'd gone with them once, given up everything to chase the dream that they'd dangled in front of him. "I don't know why they're here."

As the prisoners fell to their knees before the Loba, the wayob pressed their spears to their white chests. Vero searched their visors for hints of the faces beneath them, faces he imagined were wracked with terror. The Loba turned to Vero, then to the SEAX hovering above him. "You've been deceived, Vero."

"What are you talking about?"

"Two days ago, you submitted your SEAX to the *Daily Harbinger* tech team for routine maintenance."

Nuwairah. What did you do?

"They planted a hidden transponder. It has been transmitting your location to the United Nations Parliamentary Peacekeeper CORPS. The *Daily Harbinger* has taken a side."

"I had nothing to do with this!" Vero pleaded. "Please, don't hurt them —"

"Do you know what they are?" The Loba paced back and forth, studying the ghostly figures. "Beneath their white veils?"

"If you're looking for hostages, take me instead!" Vero stepped toward the peacekeepers, but the wolves lunged at him, snapping and snarling.

"They chose their end long ago. When they took up the white mantle."

"You may threaten us all you like," a prisoner said, in a stilted basso, their vocal modulator damaged. "But there's no escaping what's coming for you."

The confidence in the peacekeeper's voice startled Vero. What if he had it all wrong? What if it was the Loba who was in danger?

"There has to be a diplomatic solution to this," Vero blurted.

The Loba laughed. "I have survived far worse than these self-hating fools." She lifted her arm as if to strike them. Instead, she pulled off their helmets, one by one, revealing terror-stricken eyes set in brown faces. As brown as his. "They are so colonized that they are willing to die to defend the system that keeps them subservient and impotent."

The sky above them shuddered. It wasn't a thunderclap. He was sure of it.

"It's over, Aleja." The peacekeeper smirked. "This is checkmate."

In one swift motion, her heel smashed into his solar plexus. "Never call me that name!" The man crumpled at her feet, clutching his chest in agony. "Aleja is dead. Only the Loba remains."

She folded her arms. "Strip them. Paint them in our colors and drop them in the forest."

Nodding, the wayob herded the prisoners.

The Loba bared her serrated teeth. "Let's see if their accursed weapons can distinguish friend from foe."

"No! You can't leave us with *them!*" One of the prisoners shouted in stilted Spanish, a young woman from another part of the world.

"Would you rather I rip out your heart?" The Loba laughed, brandishing an obsidian dagger that had been clipped to her waist. The woman shrieked as the wayob led her down the steps of the pyramid.

"Oh, relax," the Loba sighed. "Depictions of human sacrifice are greatly exaggerated."

With a sound so deep that Vero felt it in his bones, a silver vessel deliquesced out of the clouds, slowing as it neared the pyramid. He'd seen something like this before.

Fuck.

He straightened as the Loba approached, dagger still in hand. It was the first time he saw fear in her eyes, but she quickly masked it with rage. "What's happening?" he whispered, hoping he was wrong.

As quickly as she'd turned on him, she wheeled around, holding the dagger in front of her. "You were there in Siberia with the Tsarina. You must remember the hulks clamoring through the snow, the ones she used to crush the Novemberists."

Vero pitched his face to the sky as the vessel released its cargo. A dozen hexagonal pods. Their parachutes shimmered with all the colors of the visible spectrum. He had seen these terrible beauties before. "Marionettes …"

Abey had said that the dead have no navel. Was the dream a warning?

The Loba pointed to his SEAX with the tip of her blade. "I'm afraid our interview may be cut short. But before we adjourn here, I have a few questions of my own."

The Loba approached her throne and activated a console embedded in her armrest. "Tell me, Vero Diaz, what was your grandfather's sobriquet?"

Vero shuddered, as images from his dream resurged. He could see Abey whispering to him, with that face that looked as if were carved from red sandstone. "El Indio."

A series of obsidian mirrors sprouted up from hidden cavities in the pyramid. "Were you not among the protestors in your capital of San Juan, calling for independence from America?"

Vero had been there for the marches, the sit-ins, the flag burnings and the perreo dancing in the streets, in those days before Teddy — when anything seemed possible. "I was."

The Loba pointed her weapon in the air. "Were you not one of the principal architects of the cacicazgo, a network of mountain villages that opposed Chinese occupation after Hurricane Teddy?"

She might as well have driven her dagger into his heart. He reeled as images of his former life flooded his mind. Anacaona and Yuíza and Dagüao and Alcimar and everything he had lost. The solar nets that lit their dreams. The medallas, the mañanitas he couldn't admit that he missed.

The Loba approached to within a foot of him. Breathing hard, he searched the depths of her eyes for the fire that rebirthed her, the pain that had carved her anew.

I've been reborn before.

"You came here because some part of you yearns for what I have to offer. Some part of you remembers the legacy that swims in your blood." The Loba extended her arms to him, but he looked away.

"Back on Borikén, the Cacicazgo was a fantasy. No one ever thought it was real. In school they taught us that the Taíno are extinct."

The Loba shrugged. "That's what they said about the Maya, yet here we are, alive and well, half a millennium after they arrived here, seeking our extermination."

One of the capsules landed at the edge of the clearing. Steam hissed from the pod.

"I don't know what you want from me. I'm just a journalist. I —"

"Heed the lesson Aleja failed to learn," the Loba said, pounding a fist to her chest. "A universe can be spoken into being. And you can yet speak the truth of another world, a world where the Taíno yet thrive, a world where the colonizer and his civilizational shackles no longer exist."

"I'm not some revolutionary," Vero growled.

Esa nena no sabe na. They would never follow me.

"Tell me, Vero Diaz, what happened to your sisters and your friends?" The Loba slashed the air with her dagger at the word.

He'd left and never looked back. Of course he'd wanted to. But he'd known that if he'd allowed himself to think of Anacaona and Yuíza and Dagüao he would return not just to his beloved family, but to a community that didn't value him. No, his eyes were trained on the future. There was no going back.

"What if I told you they were killed defending their homeland?" The Loba pointed her blade at the steaming pods. "From Marionettes like these?"

"Damn you!" Vero seethed, and the wolves pricked up their ears.

"You refuse to take up the mantle you were born for. But remember what I said, Mr. Diaz — sometimes the path finds us." She lunged with her dagger, and he ducked, dropping to one knee. When he recovered he found that her weapon had impaled his SEAX. White sparks still bloomed from the wound.

"I have set you free," the Loba said, lowering the blade to her side. "For all they know, you are dead by my hand." The Loba peered down at him as he kneeled like a supplicant. "Now let me tell you something about this 'career' for which you sacrificed everything. The intention was noble, perhaps, but you got it wrong. You're no journalist. You are what we call itz'aat, the scribe whose words can reshape the cosmos."

He thought of Anacaona spray painting coquís on the observatory. He thought of *La Jardinera*, a story about a modern-day saint. The thousands it inspired. And then he thought of Nuwairah and the *Daily Harbinger*. He'd run to Nuwairah to escape a call he'd been hearing his whole life. He'd run, but that voice had followed him. Sometimes the path finds us.

At the base of the pyramid, the machine stirred. Ivory filaments unraveled from the pod, thickening until they were molten pythons twining, absorbing the outer shell. The programmed matter moved with computational precision. Plastichrome plates snapped into pre-ordained sockets. The chrysalid stood to full height, towering above the canopy. Celadon eyes ignited below its crown of white spines.

Vero jumped to his feet. If his sisters were dead, he would not follow them to an early grave. "We need to leave!"

The crimson wolves snarled as the colossal automata advanced from all sides of the forest. The animals rallied to their master, who held her dagger in a reverse grip. From this height he could see that the wayob had assembled around the pyramid in great numbers, brandishing their obsidian pikes as the white hulks closed in. Screams erupted in the forest as the Marionettes lumbered closer. The wayob unleashed their smart volleys, their pikes doubling as carbines, but the weapons were of little use. Bullets sparked off the Marionettes' thick armor.

Vero paced to the edge of the platform and the Loba moved to stand beside him.

"What happened in Borikén was my fault."

One of the Marionettes recomposed its hand into the shape of a serrated blade, reducing the Loba's prized wayob to a mess of gore spattered across the lowest steps of the pyramid. Vero turned from the scene to his host, who seemed to be aglow, like the beatific saints of the Catholics she loathed.

"They called me Cacique. Our word for king."

The Loba Roja smiled, and for the first time the pull of her lips over her teeth was not terrifying. "You wrote that our lives are like trees, every choice a new branch, a new future."

Below them, the machines started climbing the stairs, their white armor stained with blood.They were taller than the four ceibas surrounding the pyramid.

"For us Maya, those four ceibas, those Yax Che, are what hold up the three worlds: the world of mortals, the world of the gods, and the underworld where the dead dwell. But they also reach through time. *Past-Present-Future.* The world that you thought lost is still within reach."

Vero retreated as the shadows of the ascending mechs darkened his world. "A second chance."

"Are you ready to begin your metamorphosis?"

Vero panted, eyes rolling from one side of the pyramid and then the other. "What must I do?"

When the Loba Roja met Vero's eyes, her look was one of excitement. "You must face death!" she shouted, and she rushed to meet their foe, dagger raised to strike. She called to him as she flew down the steps. "You must reach into the r'muxux ruchilew, the navel of the world."

Vero flinched from the edge of the pyramid as the Marionettes balled their fists. Then a rending light flashed through the clearing as the pyramid's obsidian mirrors activated, ricocheting the sun's photons into a weapon.

"Hunahapu and Xbalanque will guide you!" the Loba shouted, a red blur charging. "To a realm of fear where you will be reborn!"

The wolves leapt into the brazier, taking burning branches into their mouths. They rushed toward the roof comb, weaving through an unseen shaft. Vero hurried after them, pausing before the stone portal decorated with the fangs of a great beast.

Reach into the r'muxux ruchilew.

As Vero thrust his hand into the beast's mouth, a hidden mechanism activated. The platform spun slowly, and he caught a glimpse of the Loba as the Marionettes struck at her with their spicate arms, hitting nothing but air and light. He watched as the simulacrum she had been dissolved into what looked like mud. Unsatisfied by her false flesh, the Marionettes trained their eyes on him, a thousand celadon suns searing his heart.

You must face death.

They reached, their white claws bearing down on him as the lift activated. The world reeled. He held his breath as he plunged into a shimmering abyss.

This is what it means to rule from below.

From Xibalba, the realm of fear.

siembra | sowing

"There is a gardener at the end of the world. In the rubble, she sows seeds. In rotted soil, she dreams of sunflowers. Is hope a refusal to accept difficult truths? Is it a species of madness, a coping mechanism for those that weather oblivion? Or is it the virtue of a visionary?"

Vero Diaz, "La Jardinera," reprinted by the *Daily Harbinger*

The water in the pail sloshed over her brown hand, droplets kissing her wrists as she climbed the hill to the Casa. Above, the golden sun's reign was broken only by thin clouds, scattered islands of moisture whispering of restoration. Springing up from the wounds of the desert, the jungle was retaking the land. Like brilliant jewels, shoots of myrtle and jacaranda dappled the ochre canvas of the valley in hues of verdant green.

Margarita whistled as she walked, waving to residents who now spent their days tending amaranth, maize, and chili seedlings in the planters they had fashioned from pieces of shacks lost to months of flooding.

Toñito and Angela sprinted by her, their shrieks of laughter a

127

welcome addition to the valley's ambiance which now included the songs of motmots, the murmur of goats and cattle on the lush slopes. The twins were mirror images of their parents, Ismael and Ximena. The children, now three years old, had been born to a world ravaged by waves of mud and war. In the messy days of reconstruction, the cries of newborn children reminded Margarita and the others what was at stake — and what was possible. In the laughter of the children, they heard hope. As the valley surged into new life and the children grew, so did the resolve of the sórdidos, for now they had a collective purpose: to sow for them a future worth living and dying for. Growing up in this collective, the youngsters addressed each member of their community as a tío or tía, but Margarita enjoyed a different title.

"Ten cuidado!" Margarita warned as their unsteady feet carried them in circles near the steep ditches Ximena's team had carved to irrigate their modest fields.

"Yes, Abuela!"

Before making her way to the kitchen, where a feast was being prepared to celebrate their first harvest, Margarita followed the fern-speckled footpath to the back of the house.

Though sunken, warped, and buckled by water and time, the flower beds she and José Antonio had built years earlier had remained intact. Margarita leaned in to smell the white hibiscus that was blooming there, and then turned to Abuelo's verdant grave.

"Did you send these to us from the other side, my old friend?"

xibalba | coabey | underworld

"The Taíno say that during the day their dead dwell in seclusion, deep in a cave called Coabey, but at night their spirits, their opía, roam in search of ripe guayaba to engorge themselves ... one must be wary of impostors, of those dead that try to deceive the living, the ones without navels."

An Account of the Antiquities of the Indians, Ramón Pané, circa 1498 CE, as retold by Abey Soto de Jayuya

"Then went One Hunahpu and Seven Hunahpu, guided by the messengers as they descended along the path to Xibalba ... down steep steps ... into the House of Darkness."

Anonymous, *Popol Vuh*, circa 1550 CE

In the dark of Xibalba, he was reborn. Become the Jurakán. Bare-chested, the scars where his breasts had been were faintly visible beneath whorls of achiote pigments that striped his body and face. *The living storm.* A frond of pleated kapok fibers flowed from his waist. *The spiral that is reckoning.* The silver-streaked twists of his hair fell past his hips. *The great sower.* She rested the corona atop his head, its crest

129

of cotinga feathers illuminating the sepulcher with every hue of hibiscus and sea. *You must be the cloud that melts into the dawn, the herald of the rising sun.*

And so he was anointed, Agüeybaná, cacique of the Solar Cacicazgo of the Taíno resurgent.

He walked along a raised outcrop of limestone, between two underground rivers, one hued red with sediments, the other chalky with lime. They stood at the end of each tributary, her chuchqajaw priests, their conical heads gleaming in the milky light. He eyed their staves as he passed them, wrought from the bones of the Caudillo's victims.

She waited for him by an obsidian plinth, her red wolves seated at her feet.

"Their fleet gathers in the Atlantic," said the Loba Roja behind a mask of buffed malachite. She inserted an ilb'al crystal into the plinth, activating the display. "My chuchqajaw have extrapolated their trajectory. They mean to make landfall in the north, using the old Spanish fort, El Morro, as a staging ground for the invasion."

Agüeybaná frowned at the ranks of white dirigible-galleons surging over the turquoise waters. "Let them gather."

She peered at him with interest. "My chuchqajaw stand ready to unleash their Cohoba sorcery upon the sea."

Agüeybaná leaned into the projected map. "Tell them to hold their positions for now."

The Loba nodded, folding her arms.

"Soon enough, the dreaming stones will punish the wicked for their insolence." Agüeybaná reached over to the spherical shell of the SEAX resting on an obsidian plinth. "But first, they must know who they are up against."

The eyes of the Loba brightened, visible through the slits in her mask. "Xibalba has taught you well, Heart of Sky."

Agüeybaná nodded, rebooting his SEAX companion, watching

its cracked glass eye flicker with blue light. "I must rekindle their fear of ghosts. I will give them the retribution that for centuries they feared might come."

"The wrath of Guabancex, cemí of the Jurakán, the living storm." The Loba traced the spiral etched on his skin.

"I will show them that our myths live on in us," said Agüeybaná as he initiated the broadcast.

• • •

cosecha | harvest

"Are saints real? Maybe we evolved to need heroes. Because they inspire. Because they are what we can never be. And this is the problem with heroes. We seldom consider their humanity. We look past the blemishes that make them human, so that they can be what we require them to be."

Vero Diaz, "La Jardinera", reprinted by the *Daily Harbinger*

In the kitchen, as the afternoon waned, Margarita prepared red-corn tortillas. Behind her, the hinges of the main door squeaked.

"Am I invited to dinner?"

Margarita looked up from her masa to find Juaco, wearing a rumpled suit and a sombrero. His face looked more gaunt than she remembered.

Juaco removed his hat. "You've really made something of this place."

Margarita wiped the masa from her hands and ran to kiss his cheeks. "I knew you would come someday."

Juaco seated himself on the stool beside her, eyeing her mess of corn flour and fritters.

"You look wiser, joven." Returning to her work, Margarita formed perfect discs with the palm of her hand.

"It's been an eventful three years." Juaco scratched the stubble that darkened his light skin.

Margarita handed him a tostada. "I need a taster — I think this masa might be too sweet."

Juaco's eyes closed as he bit into the red tostada oozing with cheese and beans. "Riquísimo. It's got that perfect crisp."

Margarita threw another batch of tortillas on the griddle. "And how is the palace?"

"You mean the Green Zone?" Juaco laughed. "*This* is the Green Zone now. The UN packed up and left. The spheres are gone. No one wants them here after their lies came to light."

Margarita flipped the tortillas. "And the Loba Roja?"

"There is peace, for now."

"Good." Margarita wiped her hands with a wet cloth. "Let's enjoy it while it lasts."

Juaco looked down at his plate, at the half-eaten tostada.

"But you are not at peace, are you joven?"

"At the Quetzal camp, there was barely any food." He picked at the tostada, considered the grease on his fingers.

"The hydrophage killed everything that grew."

Juaco nodded. "They had to make decisions, prioritize certain prisoners over others." His hands trembled and he twisted them in his lap. "I heard the gunshots, when they killed off the old and the sick and the weak."

Again, he picked up and set down the tostada. When he spoke he would not meet Margarita's eyes. "I was so hungry I took another boy's rations when he was sleeping."

Margarita covered his hand with hers.

"The next day, he told the officers that there was a thief among us," Juaco buried his face in his hands. "They blamed a teenager we called Flaco. A kid with a defiant streak. They took him outside and shot him and I said nothing. I let him die because I was hungry and alone and selfish and a coward who wanted to sleep with a full belly."

Margarita rounded to his side of the counter, rubbed his back. "To be hungry is to be human, mijo."

Juaco clenched his fists. "I've spent every day since trying to bring the Caudillo to justice — trying to atone for my weakness." His red-dened eyes were bright and clear. "Flaco died and I lived. I robbed him of a life so that I could have a second chance."

This is who you have been grieving.

"I wanted to make things right," he said, turning from Margarita, masking his tears. "So I sought out the boy's family. But there are no records — the Caudillo erased him from history. Just like my parents." Juaco fought to keep his voice steady. "There is no one I can ask for forgiveness. No one I can ask for guidance. Except for you."

Margarita shook her head. "You don't need to be forgiven. You were just a boy. What you must do is learn how to forgive yourself."

"What if I can't?" Juaco drummed the counter with his fingers. "I still fight for him, the dead boy that should have been me. I fight because I don't deserve peace."

Margarita returned to the grill heaping the last of the tostadas on a tray. "Everyone deserves peace."

"Even Gonzalo?"

Margarita nodded slowly. She covered the tray of steaming tostadas with a cloth to keep them warm.

"You look like him," Margarita said after a long silence. "My Bastian. How I imagine he might look if he'd had the chance."

Juaco lowered his head. "I wish I could bring him back."

"God spared us for a reason. I believe we were always meant to find each other, so that we could remember."

"Remember what?"

"What a family is."

"But that's just it, Margarita, I can't remember. I was just a boy when this started. They're strangers to me now, the family the Caudillo took from me. I can barely remember their faces." Juaco stared at her for a long while, his eyes welling with tears. "And I'm so broken, Margarita. I'm so goddamned broken —"

The boy sobbed and she held him, like she'd done for her own children when the world had been too much for them to bear, the way his mother might have done for him if she were still alive. "You have a home here with us, mijo. Here in this place where the broken come to be mended, where deserts learn how to become green again."

Juaco helped Margarita carry tostadas and fritters outside to set them on the table where the residents were already gathered at the direction of José Antonio. Juaco sat with Margarita, and the twins sat across from them, Ismael and Ximena on either side.

"Thank you for this delicious feast, Abuelita," Toñito said, his smiling mouth already shiny with the oil from a stolen fritter. "May I have the flan now?"

"Corazón, you have to wait until after dinner," Margarita scolded. She studied the little boy's bronze face as it soured with disappointment. Then, bursting into a joyous cackle, she served him a tiny piece of flan, heaping a few spoonfuls of lemon-zested caramel atop his sliver of sweet custard.

"But today is a blessed day," Margarita began. Toñito's face was alight with joy as he tasted the flan. "Today is a miracle."

Then it was Juaco that led them in prayer, and it was Juaco that served the throngs gathered. And in that moment, as they ate tostadas and fritters and flan and plantain stew together, she realized that they were no longer sórdidos. They had been reborn, renacidos, and in the few empty chairs remaining she imagined Abuelo and her Roberto. She imagined little Bastian and her girls, and she felt their warmth as she dreamed she would when she joined them on the other side. As the sun dipped beneath the horizon, marbling the maize stalks and the saplings and the chaya blossoms with golden light, Margarita ate dinner with her family.

••••

chi releb'al q'ij | where the sun emerges

"In guaitiao, our Caciques received the covered people as blood kin. In guaitiao, they were welcomed and showered with the riches of our archipelagos. Everywhere except for the high mountain of Borikén, where my father, Cacique Hayuya, forbade them from entering. For the All-Mother Atabey warned him of the long darkness they would bring to our people of the sun. Only after twenty-four generations of slumber would their goeiz awaken so they might reclaim their lands for our eldest cemí, Yucahú Bagua Maórocoti."

The Prophecy of Aura Surey, a sixteenth century oral tradition, as retold by Abey de Jayuya

The shore was a mausoleum. Husks of frayed palms were strewn upon the beaches like the bones of mythical giants. Iridescent shards of plastichrome dappled the sands, the scattered remains of the United Nations' armada carried ashore on a dark surf. He strode over the debris, mourning the bodies of fish and pelicans and iguanas he found in the stagnant tidepools Hurricane Guabancex had left behind. Revolutions demand sacrifice, this was what the Loba had taught him. Like a snake, his Borikén felt pain as it molted.

Agüeybaná pushed into the island's interior, past felled trees and crumbling islands of asphalt from highways long reclaimed by the elements. His sojourn brought him deep into the mountains, where the jungle still dripped with mud as black as tar. There was no green to be found in this ruined world.

Not yet.

On the second day, he reached the observatory. Reduced to its foundations, the arc of the satellite dish was furry and chartreuse with moss. In the mud there were footprints. Plantain peels. Charcoal. Discarded batteries. They had been here recently. He prayed to the All-Mother Atabey that Xbalanque had found them. The lupine had been brought to the island in advance of the storm, to warn what was left of the Cacicazgo.

On the third day, he trekked past their old yucayeke, where he found fragments of solar panels and the remains of tents and tarps strewn over the barren branches of the ceibas that had survived the Guabancex's ferocity. He howled in despair, stumbling upon the remains of their old dujos, the broken plastic chairs for children they'd sat on as they planned their raids and war-games.

By dusk, he reached the remains of his grandfather Abey's hut, where the gourd with his ashes still defiantly clung to its perch on the wall. Scattered on the floor he found Abey's old dreaming stones and a y-shaped pipe he used to sniff cojóbana seeds. This was the sorcery he had sown into his Jurakán. A spell he hoped would break the minds of his foes and liberate those of his allies.

If they weren't already dead, Guabancex killed them. I failed. Unless …

Agüeybaná reached for the pipe, filling it with the pale snuff of Cohoba he found in a phial on the ground. He inhaled deeply, sinking into the space between the cemís' dreams, stumbling into the night as a somnambulist. If there were survivors, there was only one place they might have gone. The place where Abey brought him and his sisters as children. A place that smelled of guano and writhed with colorful insects. A place as dark and damp as Xibalba. The mouth of the Taíno underworld, where opía, the ancestor spirits, reside. Coabey.

The stars bloomed as he sloshed through a paludal landscape where dead things bobbed. A forest turned to swamp when the dam at Lake Guajataca burst. With each sopping step, his feet grew wearier. Mosquitos and biting flies nibbled at him, reminding him that he was still mortal. He peered up at the constellations to reorient himself, but found that the ground beneath his feet was disappearing. He waded through a nightsea of blue braziers, warm with the light of his ancestors. They spoke to him. His entire matriline whispering to him from the shores beyond the turey, the sky beyond the sky. And then he appeared, his beloved Abey — a mirage morphing with the tears that gathered in his eyes.

The Taíno live on in you. Walk with them to the place where the sun emerges.

Minutes slid into hours as he hiked, guided by the susurrations of the caciques that had come before. Just as the black sky softened, he found his quarry. A cave. Nestled in the grooves of a jagged karst promontory. Even in the dim blue of the gloaming he could see the entrance: a wound in the rock, limestone stalactites glittering like wet bones. From that maw he heard the skittering of pebbles, claws on rock, and a crimson shape splashing through the marsh.

"Xbalanque!"

The beast whined giddily, colliding with his leg in violent affection, spreading mud as it nuzzled him. Breaking away from his slobbery greeting, Xbalanque barked and started toward the cave. Behind him, the world warmed as cerise spindles of sunlight bored through the leafless canopy, revealing the throngs gathered at the cave's entrance.

Survivors.

They gasped as the sun bloomed behind him, its fire tingling his skin as it crept up from the underworld. With murmurs of recognition, they filtered out of the cave to behold him as he was, his bare chest and arms streaked with mud and red paint, a nagua of kapok fibers around his waist. But where he had once felt shame, he now felt pride.

"Vero?"

This was not the voice of a distant ancestor. His heart hammering in his chest, he searched for the source of the sound. Then he saw her, a figure standing in front of a towering ceiba whose leaves and branches looked unscathed. It was fitting, to find her there before such a resilient thing. Ceibas were there before the Spanish, the Americans, the Chinese, and the UN, and he knew they would outlast them all. Past-Present-Future.

"Vero?"

The years had coarsened Yuíza's face, but her amber eyes still burned bright. Some people refused to be broken by the world. Or Marionettes, for that matter.

"Not anymore." He grinned as she stroked the paint swirled about his forehead.

She leapt into his arms, and when he felt another set of limbs wrapping around him from behind, he turned to find Dagüao. His hair was even longer than before, a wispy beard softening his chin.

-You need a bath,- Dagüao signed, his nose wrinkling in disgust.

-And you need a shave,- Agüeybaná countered.

They laughed together for a moment as more survivors gathered to behold the familiar stranger.

-I thought you had forgotten us.- Dagüao's eyes narrowed with sudden severity.

Agüeybaná's heart caught in his throat. -I'm sorry.-

"Cacique." Anacaona stepped out of the crowd, the twists of her hair almost identical to his own, her streaks of gray mirroring his. Her face was a placid, unreadable mask. But she was his himagua, his twin,

140

and he could tell that the years had been cruel to her, that the burden of leadership had taken its toll.

"I prefer Agüeybaná," he told them, making the sign for -great sun- to Dagüao.

-Great Sun,- Dagüao repeated, smiling as he looked out at the dawn.

"Ana," he started, grabbing his sister's shoulders. "I should never have left. I should —"

She put her finger over his mouth. "You are here now, hermanito."

He lowered himself to the ground in genuflection before her. "In the absence of the sun, you were their light."

Anacaona lifted him up. "It doesn't have to be like that."

Dagüao made the sign for -king-.

Agüeybaná thought of the four dujos, and Abey's stories of the mischievous quadruplets who made the world-sea by spilling their grandfather's prized gourd. -We are all king,- he signed.

From the cave someone retrieved a pandereta and a cuatro. Then came Don Brizuela's voice over the drumming and whining strings, singing an old jíbaro tune that Abey used to listen to on his radio. One by one, their bodies were taken by the rhythm. But this was just a celebration, not the *areito* he was planning. That sacred dance would have to wait until after they had rebuilt their Cacicazgo, until after they had gathered their kin from the archipelagos, in Higüey, Xaragua, Xaymaca, Ciboney, and Guanahatabey. This is how they would remake the Caribbean as the Loba had done with the Yucatán.

Above, the sun was rising, a carmine-white halo over a brown world. A world on the brink of molting.

"Come, family," said Agüeybaná, threading his sisters' hands through his. "Let us enjoy the light of our sun."

=

postscript

In 1492, a storm named Cristóbal Colón made landfall in the
Caribbean, inaugurating a brutal era of Spanish imperial rule for
Indigenous Caribbeans under the Encomienda labor system. The
few Taínos and Kalinagos that survived the genocide, rape, disease, and
famine brought on by the Spaniards were driven into hiding or forced
to assimilate to Christianity, amounting to the irretrievable loss of their
languages and many of their customs.

In the Yucatán, Maya peoples continued to experience dispossession of their lands, forced assimilation, and genocide by the "republics"
that succeeded the Spanish Empire. Following an armed coup d'état
backed by the United States government in 1954, the stage was set for
a civil war in Guatemala (1960-1996) and the rise of a real-life
Caudillo, José Efraín Ríos Montt, who killed nearly two hundred thousand Maya people in what is known as the silent genocide. In Mexico, a
similar dynamic of Indigenous oppression resulted in the Zapatista
Uprising in 1994, an unthinkable episode in history that continues to
inspire Indigenous movements and coalitions around the world.

Today, the people of Borikén remain subjects of American
Empire with no federal representation; their economic destiny is tied to

an unelected fiscal board known as the Junta. Under their watch, a housing and infrastructure crisis is unfolding, rapidly displacing Boricuas from their ancestral lands. But there is hope. After Hurricane María in 2017, greater numbers of Boricuas are identifying with their African and Taíno heritage. Many are openly criticizing the United States Government. The independence movement is experiencing a resurgence on a scale unseen since the 1950s. Boricuas are beginning to see Borikén as deeply theirs. In 2019, sitting Governor Ricardo Rossello was forced to resign after millions descended upon the capital demanding his resignation. The Cacicazgo is awakening.

Today, the Yucatán and the Caribbean regions are among the world's most vulnerable to climate change. Their fate is tied to yours.

glosario | glossary

波多黎各 Puerto Rico (Simplified Mandarin)

你好 Hello (Simplified Mandarin)

Agüeybaná Supreme Chief of Borikén, killed in battle against Spanish in 1511 (Taíno Arawak)

Anacaona Chieftess of Xaragua, hanged by the Spanish at a peace banquet in 1504 (Taíno Arawak)

anacaona golden flower (Taíno Arawak)

areito ceremonial dance (Taíno Arawak)

baalche' hardwood tree; its bark is used to make a sacred beverage (Yucatec Maya)

batzil'op those of the original word (Tzeltal Maya)

behike shaman or medicine man (Taíno Arawak)

bohio round thatch hut made of plant fibers (Taíno Arawak)

bomba traditional dance/musical genre of West African origin (Spanish)

Buluc Chabtan war deity (Yucatec Maya)

cacique / kasike chief (Taíno Arawak)

cacica hispanicized term for a Taíno chieftess (Spanish, derived from Taíno Arawak)

cacicazgo chiefdom (Taíno Arawak)

casabe starchy flatbread made from manioc/cassava (Taíno Arawak)

ceiba Silk Cotton Tree / Kapok (Taíno Arawak)

cemí (also **zemí**) deities housed in stone (Taíno Arawak)

Chaak rain deity (Yucatec Maya)

ch'aqa palo across the sea; to the east (K'iche' Maya)

chaya white-flowered shrub native to the Yucatán (Yucatec Maya/Spanish)

chilam balam voice of the Jaguar; anointed sages (Yucatec Maya)

chi releb'al q'ij where the sun emerges; in the east (K'iche' Maya)

chipilín flavorful herb used in Mesoamerican cuisine (Nahuatl)

chuchqajaw keepers of tradition; spiritual leaders (K'iche' Maya)

creyente practitioner of Santería (Spanish)

coabey underworld (Taíno Arawak)

Cohoba divination ritual; hallucinogenic snuff made from Cojóbana seeds (Taíno Arawak)

conuco raised mound used for agriculture (Taíno Arawak)

coquí tree frog onomatopoetically-named for its distinct mating call (Spanish)

copal aromatic tree resin used as incense in Mesoamerican cultures (Nahuatl)

Dagüao Chief of Naguabo, destroyed the Spanish City of Santiago (Taíno Arawak)

dujo tiny ceremonial throne for Chiefs and Nobles (Taíno Arawak)

egun ancestor spirits; bones (Yoruba)

goeiz spirits of the living (Taíno Arawak)

Guayaba tropical fruit, Lord of the Dead (Taíno Arawak)

guanín gold-red metal; necklace worn by a Chief (Taíno Arawak)

guaitiao customary greeting, establishing fictive blood kin relation (Taíno Arawak)

guajiro/a/e term that refers to countrymen in a rural context, esp. Cuba (Taíno Arawak)

guineo banana, refers to its West African origin in Guinea (Spanish)

güiro percussion instrument made from hollowed gourd (Taíno Arawak)

himagua twin (Taíno Arawak)

huipil Traditional blouse with rhombus pattern (Mayan Languages)

Hunhapu One of the Maya Hero Twins (K'iche' Maya)

Ifá priests (Yoruba)

iguana a herbivorous lizard indigenous to the Americas (Taíno Arawak)

ilb'al instrument of sight; crystal used in rituals (K'iche' Maya)

itulu funerary rites (Yoruba)

itz'aat sage or scribe (K'iche' Maya)

Ix Chel moon goddess / deity of textiles (Yucatec Maya)

jaba sack (Taíno Arawak)

jamaca hammock (Taíno Arawak)

jíbaro sometimes used as derogatory slur; refers to rural folk in Puerto Rico (Kalinago Arawak)

jícara gourd (Taíno Arawak)

Jurakán Deity known as Heart of Sky/ tropical cyclone (Taíno Arawak/Ki'che'/Yucatec Maya)

k'ulaj welcome (K'iche' Maya)

K'uk'ulkan the feathered serpent deity (Yucatec Maya)

ladino person of mixed ancestry; often Christianized; not culturally Indigenous (Spanish)

le kiäqa utiw the red wolf; the red coyote (K'iche' Maya)

lobo/a wolf; a derogatory racial epithet for a person with mixed ancestry (Spanish)

macana war club (Taíno Arawak)

maraca percussive musical instrument (Taíno Arawak)

naboria peasant class (Taíno Arawak)

nagua cotton loincloth traditionally worn by men (Taíno Arawak)

ñame sweet potato (Taíno Arawak/Bambara)

nasa fibrous net used to hunt fish (Taíno Arawak)

nitaíno noble class (Taíno Arawak)

obiwayza Style of Vejigante mask made from coconut shells (Disputed origin; likely Yoruba/Taíno Arawak)

opía spirits of the dead (Taíno Arawak)

Opiyel Guobiran canine deity (Taíno Arawak)

orishas deity-spirits (Yoruba)

Perreo an *expressive* genre of dance — just look it up on YouTube (Spanish)

poleo wild mint (Spanish)

saco traditional coat worn by men (Spanish)

Santería Syncretic West African & Christian Religion (Spanish)

t'ho tropical bird related to Kingfishers; also called mot mot (Yucatec Maya)

tepew honorific used to address a Sovereign (Nahuatl/K'iche' Maya)

Tulan the fabled place that exists 'across the sea' (K'iche' Maya)

turey sky, the heavens (Taíno Arawak)

utiw coyote or wolf (K'iche' Maya)

wayob or **way** were-beings (K'iche' Maya)

Xbalanque One of the Maya Hero Twins (K'iche Maya)

xibalba underworld (K'iche' Maya)

xtabentún Mesoamerican morning glory plant (Yucatec Maya)

x' takay yellow-bellied flycatcher indigenous to the Yucatán (Yucatec Maya)

xukul nicte flame of the forest tree; an African tulip (Yucatec Maya)
ya'axché Silk Cotton Tree/Kapok (Yucatec Maya)
yuca manioc or cassava, a tropical tuber (Taíno Arawak)
Yuíza Legendary Chieftess of Jaymanío (Taíno Arawak)
Yucahu Bagua Maorócoti the one without beginning; fatherless; eldest;
    supreme being (Taíno Arawak)
yucayeke village (Taíno Arawak)

references

The book of chilam balam of Chumayel. Vol. 523. Translated by Ralph Roys.
    Washington, DC: Carnegie Institution of Washington, 1933.

Popol Vuh: The sacred book of the Maya. Vol. 1. Translated by Allen J.
    Christenson. University of Oklahoma Press, 2007.

Roosevelt, Theodore. *Winning of the west, pt. 1-4.* Vol. 6. Putnam, 1889.

acknowledgments

Stories are like plants. They must be sown, watered, and pruned over many seasons. If you're lucky, you might get something that bears fruit or sweet-smelling flowers. Most tales begin with a seed, a flicker of inspiration that sends you to your computer or the nearest pen and paper to scribble a tangle of words, ideas, or lines of dialogue. *Sordidez* began with a photograph: the home of my late grandmother in Guaynabo, Puerto Rico. The place where as a youth I chased chickens and lizards and ate mangos from our trees. A place greener than anything I would ever see spending most of my life in snowy New England. But the photograph I saw looked nothing like the green wonderland I remembered so vividly from my childhood. Instead, I was met with an image of brown ruin, as if the jungle had been torched to cinder. I saw this photograph in October of 2017, in the tumultuous weeks after Hurricane María made landfall.

When I visited the island the following March, I found that green shoots were already sprouting in the wounds carved by María. The people too, were healing, albeit imperfectly. Though many had fled the island, and many more would follow, those who stayed looked after each other — clearing roads, rebuilding homes, cooking meals, and pooling resources to survive the aftermath of the greatest natural disaster in American history. Even as their infrastructures and governments failed them, everyday Puerto Ricans rose up to take action. These heroes, caretakers, and visionaries are Doña Margarita. They are the light that refuses to dim. My wish is that *Sordidez* honors these heroes, their extraordinary sacrifices, their compassion, and their ongoing struggle for liberation. For as the land heals so must its people. *Puerto Rico se levanta.*

Writing, like gardening, is not a solitary act. It takes a cacicazgo to write a book. While many of the people who helped shape this manuscript know me, there are others who remain unaware of how they influenced *Sordidez*. Among them is Dr. Kirsten Weld, author of *Paper Cadavers*, a searing history of the Guatemalan Civil War pieced together from crumbling archives that survived decades of brutal repression and genocide; Dr. Vera Candiani, author of *Dreaming of Dry Land*, which chronicles the real-world inspiration for the Caudillo's hydrophage, the Desagüe of Tenochtitlan; Drs. Sherina Feliciano-Santos and Christina Marie González for their careful research and writing on contemporary Indigenous communities in the Caribbean; Jose Barreiro, activist, journalist, and elder of the Nación Taina, best known for his remarkable historical novel, *Taíno*; and Dr. Shariann Lewitt, for her amazing science fiction workshop class at MIT and for telling me *Sordidez* "wanted" to be more than a short story.

It is a difficult task to write about cultures and communities that are at once familiar and strange. As a child of diaspora, my perspective and imagination are limited. I could never have written this book if I had not had the chance to reside in or visit the places that appear in *Sordidez*. Throughout the course of my research, I interviewed many people who I hope ground my worldbuilding in *Sordidez*. I wish to thank: my cousin, Laura Adorno Monserrate, for helping me navigate life in Puerto Rico and for believing in me when I didn't believe in myself; Liliana Riva Palacio and her amazing team at Proyecto Concentrarte in Ciudad México and Chiapas; Doña Gladys and the people of Miguel Hidalgo, for their incredible hospitality and their beautiful vision of the world; Miguel Sobaoko Koromo, a Taíno Behike whose spiritual counsel inspired me and grounded my writing; my partner, Jia Hui Lee, for his care, compassion, and patience, as I worked through many drafts of this novella; my dearest friends, Jon Arsenault, Joe Le, Nerrishia Bodwell, Liz Malone, Nate Perreira, Nico

Avallone, Sam Faer, McKynzie Bair, Elena Sobrino, Maria Sobrino, Beth Semel, Alex Mosher, and Allison Shufelt, for always cheering me on and listening to my story synopses; my Nashoba Brook Bakery writing group (Sarah Pinto, Caitrin Lynch, Casey Golomski, and Elizabeth Ferry), for teaching me how to be a better reader and writer; my graduate cohort G.L.M. Robbins, A. Rewegan, A.R. Sorokin; Dr. Allen J. Christenson, for granting me permission to include epigraphs from his stunning English translation of the *Popol Vuh* from K'iche'; my mentors, Stefan Helmreich, Graham Jones, Heather Paxson, Janet McIntosh, Sharon Stephens, James Hayford, Rosemary Gianno, Katherine Tirabassi, Ron Tunning, LP Kindred, and Beth Arsenault, for sharing their wisdom with me and supporting my writing habit (sometimes at the expense of other more pressing matters); my sensitivity readers and collaborators, Felix Seidel, Doris Alcantara Quinones, Ariel Baker Gibbs, and Jason Bartles; Ben Arsenault for reading *Sordidez* when it was just a short story; Ren Hutchings (@voidcricket) for reading through the many drafts of this project and providing crucial editorial feedback; Jessica Veter; Paulina Niño (IG @Paulinaninoarte) for her astonishing painting, "La Jardinera," which I am proud serves as the cover art for this book; Priscilla Bell Lamberty for sharing my passion for #TaínoFuturism and bringing my characters to life with her beautiful and evocative concept art; my Taíno ancestors, especially bisabeula (great grandmother) Alejandrina Martinez Rosa de Condé, a renowned healer who made the best arroz con leche in the universe; my late sister, Michelle Gonzalez Green, who spent her last days tracing her Afro-Taína lineage; my parents, for teaching me how to care for others; and my seventeen nephews and nieces, for making my world happier and louder; also Chloe the Hound and Horsie. Finally, this book would be nothing without Selena Middleton, the editor whose tireless support and encouragement brought my lifelong dream of publishing a book to fruition.

about the author

Photo by Jon Sachs

E.G. Condé (he/him/Él) is a queer diasporic Boricua writer of speculative fiction. Condé is one of the creators of "Taínofuturism," an emerging artistic genre that imagines a future of Indigenous renewal and decolonial liberation for Borikén (Puerto Rico) and the archipelagos of the Caribbean. His short fiction appears in *Anthropology & Humanism, If There's Anyone Left, Reckoning, EASST Review, Tree & Stone Literary Magazine, Sword & Sorcery, Solarpunk Magazine*, and *FABLE: An Anthology of Sci-Fi, Horror & The Supernatural*. He is also an anthropologist of technology and digital sustainability advocate (as Steven Gonzalez Monserrate). When he isn't conjuring up faraway universes, you might find him hiking through sand dunes or playing 2D JRPGs from the 1990s. Follow his writing at www.egconde.com or on social media via @CloudAnthro on Twitter.

YOU MAY ALSO LIKE

these Stelliform Press titles by Indigenous authors.

Lush worldbuilding and humor buoy this sometimes challenging best-friends-save-the-world underwater fantasy novella.

A queer Mi'kmaw artist struggling after the death of her father faces unimaginable transformation. A new novella by an emerging Indigenous author. Coming October 2023.

STELLIFORM PRESS

Earth-focused fiction. Stellar stories.
Stelliform.press.

Stelliform Press is shaping conversations about nature and our
place within it. We invite you to join the conversation by leaving a
comment or review on your favorite social media platform. Find
us on the web at www.stelliform.press and on Twitter,
Instagram, Facebook @StelliformPress, and Mastodon
@StelliformPress@mastodon.online.

3 1270 00925 1721

CPSIA information can be obtained
at www.ICGtesting.com
Printed in the USA
BVHW061450050723
666787BV00004BB/69

9 781777 682361